The Bird Children

Barbara Spencer

Matador
5 Weir Road
Kibworth Beauchamp
Leicester LE8 0LQ, UK
Tel: (+44) 116 279 2299
Fax: (+44) 116 279 2277
Email: books@troubador.co.uk
Web: www.troubador.co.uk/matador

ISBN 978 1848766 914

British Library Cataloguing in Publication Data.
A catalogue record for this book is available from the British Library.

Typeset in 12pt Garamond by Troubador Publishing Ltd, Leicester, UK
Printed and bound in the UK by TJ International Ltd, Padstow, Cornwall

Matador is an imprint of Troubador Publishing Ltd

To Aletia Melanie whose knowledge of
ancient languages is beyond parallel

ALSO BY BARBARA SPENCER

For Children

Scruffy

A Dangerous Game of Football

For Teens

Running

Chapter One

Homeward Bound

The coach carrying the team of young footballers back to Birmingham hit a pothole, jolting Jack awake. He had been sound asleep, his head pressed against the window pane, really tired after four days at spring training camp. He elbowed Rob, dozing in the seat next to him, his dark curly head slumped on his chest.

'What are our chances of making the team for Morocco?'

Rob groaned. 'And you woke me up to ask me that. I was having such a great dream too.' He pulled a bottle of water out of his rucksack and took a sip. 'For the ten-millionth time – Andy is a definite, you are a probable, and me – well, that's anybody's guess.'

At that moment shouts of, 'Shut-up, you lot, and listen will you,' floated down the coach. Tim Woods, the team captain, climbed to his feet; his fair hair so fiercely gelled, he resembled someone who had recently escaped the clutches of a hungry, blood-sucking vampire. 'Who's running the sweepstake this year?'

'You are,' came a chorus of voices.

'What's it in aid of?' Gary called from the front row, his dark hair plaited in small dreadlocks. He knelt up on the seat, oblivious to the notice above him advising passengers to buckle-up, whenever the coach was in motion.

'Us, of course,' half-a-dozen boys bellowed back.

'That's okay then. Count me in, but not Bram – he's not allowed to gamble.'

Bram's head emerged beside him, his doleful face framed by the patka he wore for football. 'But it's okay in't it, if I 'elp Gary? 'E's useless on 'is own.'

'Okay then,' Tim agreed. Taking a notebook out of his rucksack, he tore out any remaining clean pages waving them in the air. 'In that case, I need a quid from everyone – and no credit. And don't forget to write your name on it this year, Petey, I'm not a mind-reader.'

'Can you lend me a pound, Rob?' Andy, in the row behind, leaned forward slipping his hand through the gap between the seats.

Rob scowled. 'That makes five you owe me.' He fished in his pocket pulling out a pound coin. 'Mind I get it back.'

Andy, his round face attempting to look concerned and failing miserably, jotted the figure down on a scrap of paper. 'That's five for you, plus …'

'Three for me,' Jack said.

'I got that,' Andy sounded indignant. 'Good job my birthday's coming up, otherwise I'd have to file for bankruptcy.'

Jack unbuckled his seat belt. Squeezing past Rob, he headed for the front of the coach. Grabbing some sheets of paper from Tim, he handed them back.

'Can we have some music?' he said to the driver.

The coach driver checked his rear-view mirror, suddenly registering that any number of boys were milling about at the back of his coach.

'That lot's supposed to be belted in,' he muttered. 'I'll get it in the neck if anyone gets hurt. What are they doing, anyway?'

Jack perched on the seat next to him, fascinated by the view through the huge windscreen. The motorway was busy with evening traffic and a continuous stream of vehicles swished past.

'It's the sweepstake. We have to choose our dream team for the

Morocco trip. Whoever gets closest wins the lot, or a share if there's a draw – obviously.'

'Nice.' The driver leaned forward sliding a tape into the machine. 'But tell that lot to sit down, all right?'

Jack wandered back down the coach noticing that Mr Slinger, their new assistant coach, had woken up.

'I suppose you wouldn't like to put us out of our misery and tell us the team for the trip?'

Mr Slinger yawned sleepily. 'Not a chance. You've been a member of this squad, Jack, long enough to know that Peter Barnabus would have my guts for garters, if I did.'

'Oh go on, Slingshot,' a voice from nearby called.

Mr Slinger twisted sideways peering between the neck rests. 'Slingshot? Is that what I'm reduced to?'

'It's your new nickname, sir,' Leonard said from the row behind. 'We decided on it last night. It's a … it's a …'

'Compliment?' Mr Slinger suggested hopefully.

'Yes, sir.' Leonard waggled his head up and down eagerly. 'We gave it to you because you hit the baseball out of the field.'

Mr Slinger laughed. 'You forgot to mention the bit about the ball smashing through the windscreen of a car, or were you being polite?'

'Er …'

'He forgot,' Jack came to his team-mate's rescue. 'And Tim's new name is Tiger.' Mr Slinger appeared puzzled. 'Tiger …Woods,' Jack explained, 'because he drove the golf ball furthest.'

'I see-e.'

'But Leonard's still a nerd,' a voice shouted.

'That's not fair,' Andy called out, overhearing. 'Leonard's not half-bad now.'

Leonard beamed.

'I deeply regret not attending your midnight feast, choosing instead to go to bed like a sensible person,' said Mr Slinger. 'Think what I missed.'

'We'll invite you again next year, sir,' Jack said cheekily.

'And we're thinking of changing Andy's name to Porcupine,' Tim called.

'Why?'

'Der,' chorused half-a-dozen anonymous voices.

Mr Slinger grinned good-humouredly. 'Listen, you lot. I may have lost a few brain cells with age but my ball-kicking skills are still superior to yours – so enough of the cheek.'

'Because anyone *that good in goal*, will definitely be a thorn in the other team's side,' Tim said.

'Or a nail in their coffin,' Rob shouted.

'Right, got it. Any other changes I need to know about?'

'Not really,' Jack shook his head.

'I say, sir, *sir*?' Petey leapt up in his seat, waving his arm to attract their coach's attention. 'Did they tell you, we used to have a prince in our team – Saleem.'

'A real Prince, seriously, Petey?'

Rob, overhearing, put down the paper he'd been scribbling his choice of names on. 'Great striker he was too, sir. Only little, but could he run! Went like the clappers.'

'So why did he quit the team?'

'Went back home,' Petey said.

Petey, whose real name was Roger Prentice, had earned his nickname because of his outrageous hairstyles; his current version having a wide, blue and maroon stripe across the back with a deep orange quiff – like some rare species of parrot.

'We never knew Saleem was a prince till after. The club did but they never let on. Jack said he wanted to be treated like one of the lads. Came from some place strange, he did.' Petey scratched his head, his quiff wobbling like a jelly. 'Sultana – that's it.'

'*Sudana, you wally.* I must have told you a million times,' Jack snorted with laughter. 'It's one of those kingdoms in the Sudan,' he said to Mr Slinger.

'Wish he was still here. I'm the only Asian left in the team now,' Bram broke in.

'How come you're from Asia, all of a sudden?' Gary popped his head back up. 'And there's me thinking you're Ebrahim Patel who lives next door, and was born in Selly Oak hospital – like me.' He raised his voice slightly. 'I say, sir, when I was born – two days after Bram – mum says he took one look at my black face and screamed blue murder.'

'*No way,*' Bram shouted over the laughter. 'Me mum says it was the other way round. When you saw *my* face, you stopped breathing altogether and turned blue. Besides, you're like me,' he said reverting to his original argument. 'You come from St. Kitts. That makes you West Indian.'

'Honestly, Bram, you really are a prize git. My *family* came from St Kitts. I was born in England – that makes me English.'

'Well, I'm still Indian,' Bram said a mulish expression on his face.

'Try living there then,' Gary scowled at his friend. 'Your Brummy accent's that strong – they'll need to use a dictionary if you tell them good morning.'

Howls of laughter swept over the group of boys.

'Are they always like this?' Mr Slinger asked.

'Yep,' Jack grinned. 'But don't try insulting Bram – only Gary's allowed to do that, and he's pretty handy with his fists. Mrs Patel told us on their second day in reception – that's the first year of primary – some kid couldn't remember Ebrahim, and called him *hymn-book* instead. Next thing Gary was belting him over the head with his book bag, screaming: *you leave him alone, Bram's my friend.*'

Mr Slinger screwed up his face.

'They were only little, sir,' Jack explained patiently. 'Besides, Gary couldn't pronounce his name either – so he's been Bram ever since. Actually, sir, is it true that Barney has a letter on file from their mums, begging that you either choose both of them for the team or neither?'

Mr Slinger eyed the warring boys with new interest. 'I'll look,' he said, his eyes twinkling.

'Bram's right. It's a pity we lost Saleem,' Rob confided as Jack sat down again. 'The team's a bit light this year.' He checked the names on his list. 'We could have done with him.'

Jack had never dared tell anyone of his visit to the little kingdom or how he had managed to rescue Saleem from his uncle, the evil Prince Saladin – not even Andy and Rob, his best mates. *They wouldn't have believed him anyway, who would?*

He glanced sideways at Rob, busily munching a pack of crisps, imagining his friend's face if he came out with the words, *You'll never guess where I went at Christmas – to Sudana to visit Saleem. Only I didn't go by plane – I went by camel.*

Of course, he'd have to explain how, in daylight, the camel was simply a wooden ornament, and it was only at night that it came alive. Then it could talk, fly, and walk through walls as if they were made of butter. The camel was also totally terrific, despite being argumentative and bad-tempered most of the time.

He had also met the camel's master, a merchant called Jacob. Except, he wasn't a merchant at all. He was a sorcerer, and a real-scary one too, who could conjure armies of fighting men out of shadows. Unbelievably weird, he always behaved in a highly suspicious manner, which left Jack wondering how he could possibly be one of the good guys – that is, until he met up with the real bad guys. Of course, having never met a sorcerer, or indeed heard of anyone who had, Jack couldn't say if being weird was part of the job description or not.

Still, if he came out with all that, at best, Rob would howl with laughter telling him to pull the other one; at worst, he would say Jack was losing his marbles or had dreamt it. And, after all this time, Jack was no longer sure it wasn't a dream.

'*Jack?*' Andy hissed.

'What?' Jack rubbed at the glass in the window, where his breath had fogged it, catching a glimpse of his reflection with its trade-mark haircut, fair and spiky, although slightly longer than it had been a few months back.

'I can only think of fourteen names.'

Rob leaned back and snatched the piece of paper Andy had stuck through the gap.

'Honestly, Andy,' he grumbled. 'How can you expect Tim to work this little lot out? It looks like a dyslexic hedgehog wrote it, using one of its quills instead of a pen.'

'I tried, all right.'

Rob handed Jack the scruffy piece of paper, a series of holes blasted in it where Andy's pencil had scribbled names out and re-written them. Sharing the sheet between them, both boys ran a finger down the list counting.

'You left your own name out, you wally,' Rob said finally. Taking Jack's pen, he printed it on the bottom of the list.

'Pass this down,' Rob kicked the seat in front and a hand appeared. Placing their three sheets in it, the boys watched them pass from row to row until they reached Tim.

Mr Slinger stood up, grabbing hold of the overhead rack as the driver leaned on the brakes. 'About twenty-minutes to go,' he called, regaining his balance. 'So – make sure you've got everything. Wastepaper, crisp packets, drink cartons – *and don't forget the chewing gum.*' He jerked his thumb behind him. 'Everything in the black bag hanging at the front of the coach, please. Now, if I'm correct you're all back to school …when …Thursday?'

'Don't remind us, sir,' Tyrone shouted.

'Okay. So then training as normal next Monday.' Talking broke out. '*By which time*,' he continued loudly, 'letters should have reached you about the trip.' Hands flew into the air. '*Wait*! Everyone gets a letter – good news or bad. If it hasn't arrived, check the board when you come in.'

The coach slowed, approaching the narrow slip road off the motorway. It swung on to the dual-carriageway heading into the centre of the city, and the dropping-off point outside Aston Villa Football Club.

Jack squinted at the clock on the panel above Gary and Bram. If a bus came along straight away, he'd be home in time for tea.

Chapter Two

An Eagerly Awaited Letter

Slightly later than usual on Monday morning and half-asleep, Jack dragged himself downstairs, a pile of books nestling under one arm. The first two days of the new school term had been ghastly, their year-eight teachers repeatedly delivering the same message – with exams less than two months away, school had just got serious.

Jack's mobile gurgled into life. Clutching the books to his chest, he was searching for it in his jacket pocket when the letter box clicked open and a flood of envelopes shot noisily through the slot. Startled, the books slid from under his arm and crashed down the stairs, landing in a heap at the bottom. Ignoring them, Jack hastily pressed the button on his mobile displaying a text from Andy.

"do u no if u r in the team? i am."

Leaving his school books where they had fallen, Jack grabbed the letters and, holding them at arms length as if they were a pair of socks he'd worn for a week, tore into the kitchen.

His mother was eating toast and marmalade, and reading the newspaper; his younger sister, Lucy, still upstairs getting ready for school. Jack dumped the letters on the table.

'Andy's in,' he announced waving his phone in her face.

She pushed his hand away. 'But you expected that, Jack. You must have told me, at least a hundred times over the past few days, what a brilliant goal-keeper he is.'

'I know,' he said through gritted teeth. 'But that means there's only fourteen places left and there's *thirty* of us wanting them.'

Folding her newspaper, Mrs Burnside flicked through the mail, separating the glossy advertising leaflets for recycling. Jack couldn't bear to look. He hid behind the cereal box, pretending to read the writing on the side of the packet – the letters blurring and running into one another.

'Hurry up!' he groaned.

'It's here, Jack,' she said after a long silence. She held up a white envelope, the club's logo embossed on it.

Jack reached out with trembling fingers, his hazel eyes miserable-looking. 'But what if it says no?'

His mother patted his hand in a comforting manner. 'Then it says *no*. But you're not going to find out unless you open it, are you?'

Anxiously, Jack slit open the envelope addressed to: *Jack Burnside, 137 Greenhill Road, Quinton, Birmingham.* The single-sheet had been typed on the club's letterhead. Feeling sick, he skimmed over the first paragraph.

'Mu-um!' He leapt to his feet knocking the pile of envelopes off the table. '*I'm in! I'm in! I'm in!*' Grabbing his mother by the waist, he whirled her round the kitchen.

'That's fantastic, Jack,' she panted when eventually he let her go. Hugging her side, she leaned against the table to get her breath back. '*Well done!* When do you go?'

Jack quickly re-read the letter. 'Er … Tuesday evening. We fly back the following … Tuesday morning. Wow! We miss a whole week of school. *Fabulous!*' he beamed. Remembering it was already Monday, he quickly added, 'Not this Tuesday though – *next Tuesday.*'

'Thank goodness for that. Well, I'm off to phone Dad to give him the good news. I told him I thought you'd make it.'

Jack's dad, an engineer, worked overseas with an oil-exploration company, and only managed a trip back to England every six months or so. At first, Jack had missed him dreadfully. They both loved football and always went to watch whenever Aston Villa was playing at home.

'How is he?' Jack tore his eyes away from the letter, the magic word Morocco pulsating like the lights of a disco, conjuring up images of fame and fortune.

'He's fine, misses us of course. Says it's no longer cold at night in the Sudan. Apparently, it's hot all the time – night and day.'

'Yeah, I know,' Jack spoke without thinking.

'What do you mean, *you know*? Come on, Jack Burnside, what have you been up to?'

Jack smiled innocently. If his mum knew of his Christmas adventure, she'd have kittens. 'Looked it up on the Internet,' he lied.

'Wow, you have been busy. First football – and now the Internet. I shall have to watch you,' his mother teased. *'And bring your washing down.* If this weather carries on,' she pointed to the rain-streaked windows, 'it'll never be dry in time.'

* * *

As Peter Barnabus had predicted, half the squad arrived on Monday night sporting soppy smiles and spent the entire briefing session patting one another on the back. The remainder wore expressions of doom and gloom, as if the world had ended and they had only just heard about it.

Barney had been coach to the junior squad at Aston Villa for so many years that even dads remembered him, although twenty years ago he had possessed more hair and less of a scowl. As usual, he tackled the subject head-on.

'I expect some of you are feeling pretty miserable right now,' he said, 'except for Brendan, who's been selected as reserve. He's busy praying that one of the team catches a mysterious illness before next week, so he can take their place.'

The joke fell flat, greeted by a mournful shuffling of feet.

'Remember lads, the side I've chosen is for this trip only. It doesn't make the slightest difference to your future. All it means is, that today – at this moment – there are fourteen boys who are fitter and happen to be playing better than some of you others. So get over your disappointment – and go out there determined to show me I was *wrong* not to choose you.'

Barney then directed his attention to the other half of the team – ignoring their beams of delight.

'You lot, don't go thinking this is a holiday. In a minute we start training and I shall expect one-hundred percent from every man in this squad. And remember, when you go abroad you are ambassadors for the club – so mind your language. Right! I'll hand you over to Tim.'

Flummoxed at having to stand up and address the team, Tim cast around for help. Not seeing any he blurted out, 'It's the result of the sweepstake – OK. Only one winner – that's Andy.'

Mouths fell open with astonishment. The names of boys most likely to win had included Tim and Jack, but definitely not Andy.

Andy beamed, his face beetroot red.

'He was the only one that got all the names right – including …' Getting into the swing of his speech, Tim paused for dramatic effect, 'Including selecting Marco for the team.'

Heads snapped round searching for Marco, who had hidden himself at the back. Chosen as striker for the Midlands Cup squad, he normally played in the under-thirteen group, and few of the older boys knew him.

'But that's not fair,' Petey burst out indignantly. 'He wasn't even at camp.'

'Only because he was on holiday in Italy with his family,' Tim said.

'Did *you* know that?' Gary accused.

Tim shook his head. 'Here you are, Andy.' He held up a bulging plastic coin-bag.

'Good job Andy doesn't have to share it then,' Rob called out. 'He's got a list of creditors as long as your arm. And, in case you're wondering, I'm first in line.'

Andy grinned. 'Right ho! Thanks – never expected it.' He waved the coin-bag in the air, his eyes glowing with delight. 'Pay you all at the end.'

'How could you think of Marco and not tell Rob and me?' Jack grumbled, on the way back to the dressing room at the end of the session.

'You saw my list.' Andy took off his gloves, slapping them against his thigh to remove any loose dirt.

'Yeah, but we couldn't read your writing,' Rob complained.

'That's your problem, nothing to do with me.'

'But why him?' Jack pursued his grievance.

'I figured the team needed another striker.'

Startled, Rob and Jack stopped dead.

'Come off it, you two.' Andy grinned, his rotund face glistening with sweat after their energetic training session. 'Wha'd'ye think I do when the ball's wandering around at the top end of the pitch? Anyway, Bram's happier playing left wing – and you never play well with Leonard, so there's no point choosing him.'

'Is it that obvious?' Jack said bitterly.

'Only if someone guesses you don't normally go around fouling your own side.'

'I didn't,' Jack protested. 'I slipped. In any case, it's not my fault if the Nerd wants to hog the ball.'

'Anyway,' Andy shrugged. 'So that left you and someone else as striker. I guessed Marco.'

Rob patted him on the back. 'You'd better watch all this thinking, Andy, you'll end up as captain if you're not careful.'

Chapter Three

A Meeting in Rabat

Fifteen eager and fit boys formed the audience in one of the small reception halls of the City Hotel. Arriving the previous night, they had seen only the airport and the sights through the window of the coach. Now, after a morning's training, they were free and a visit to the local market had been planned.

'OK, lads. Let's wrap it up there. To recap,' Barney said, his normal ferocious glare well in evidence. 'We meet in twenty minutes in the main hall. The coach will drop us at the market and pick us up, *at the same place*, in two hours. *So don't get lost.* Stay in your three's and no wandering off – *clear!* And if you're buying stuff, haggle. You should be terrific at that. I know from experience you can all argue the hind leg off a donkey. And don't carry money in your back pocket, that's begging for it to be nicked.'

Jack, Rob and Andy wandered back to their room. Andy, a frown on his usually cheerful face, dug his wallet out of his jeans pocket. Bending it in half, he tried to cram it into his shirt pocket, failing dismally.

'Here, give it to me.' Lifting up his T-shirt, Rob shoved their two wallets into a wide canvas belt round his waist. 'It's Mum's,' he growled, his face glowing with embarrassment. 'And before you say anything, I know it's not cool but she insisted. Said it might come in useful. I told her I wouldn't be seen dead wearing this thing but she stuck it in my case when I wasn't looking. And after what Barney said …' Rob grimaced, 'she might be right – but don't you dare tell any one,' he threatened his friends.

'Better than losing your money,' Jack agreed. 'But it'll make you ever so hot.' He examined the thick webbing. 'I bet the souk will be boiling.'

Jack was right. It was hot and sweaty, and horrendously noisy. A multitude of sounds besieged their eardrums. Tourists, chattering away in a variety of languages, the harsh sound of the Arab traders yelling across the stalls; camels hissed and spat, donkeys brayed, and cameras clicked. Blasts of ear-splitting noise thundered out of portable radios carried at shoulder level, cutting the voices of the chattering boys off from one other. And, above them all, the sound of birds twittering – imprisoned in cages hung high above the tented awnings.

As if that wasn't enough, a riot of colours and strange smells accosted them as they ventured deep into the warren of narrow alleys, many of them covered with rugs or garish awnings to protect the immense selection of goods from the sun.

'Jack, come here quick.' Rob tapped Jack on the shoulder, distracting his attention away from the sword-swallower. He levered his tall, skinny frame out of the squash of spectators following Rob's broad back into yet another alluring corridor. Here, his room-mates had discovered, and were inspecting, a vast array of sunglasses, watches and digital cameras, designed to tempt tourists into parting with their money.

The three boys gazed in rapturous silence, broken by the pleadings of the salesman to buy at a good price.

A hand tugged Jack's sleeve and he caught the whispered, 'My Lord Burnside?'

Startled, he spun round on his heel. Peering at him from across a pottery stall was a most extraordinary individual. Wearing the traditional full-length robe, a deep hood shielded the man's face from view, leaving only a large hooked nose and a wiry, expansive beard visible. He looked worn and haggard, his beard peppered with white; his shoulders rounded and hunched over. He stood very still regarding Jack with a gimlet eye, only his hands moving. As if they had a life of their own, they revolved endlessly round one another – like planets around the sun.

'Jacob!' Jack gasped, wondering what on earth the sorcerer was doing so far from home. Alarm bells sounded in his head. 'Is Saleem with you?' He stared wildly about him in the hope of spotting his friend's merry face.

'No, my Lord.' Jacob's eyes seemed to pierce through Jack's skull, as if they were an ex-ray machine photographing the inside of his head. 'My daughter and Prince Saleem send their best wishes, and hope that you will soon pay them a visit.'

'So what are you doing here?'

'I came to find you, my Lord.' The voice was the same, fitting into whatever role Jacob wanted; now the obsequious merchant.

'*No! You couldn't!* I mean … no one knew I was here,' Jack babbled, feeling his insides drain away as if through a massive sieve. He flicked a glance over his shoulder hoping to find Andy and Rob there, but they were engrossed examining the watches on the stall opposite and not taking any notice.

'I need your help, my Lord.'

'*No way!*' A storm of emotion rampaged through Jack, remembering how Jacob had delivered him to the palace and left him there – exactly like a trussed-up turkey – unable to make himself understood, constantly dogged by danger and fighting to stay alive. 'Besides I can't.' He pointed to his friends. 'I'm here with a football team and we're supposed to stay together. Anyway, I've got to go now. It was nice seeing you again,' he recited automatically, walking hastily across the little alleyway.

'My Lord Burnside! I need your help to locate that most

17

treacherous of all land forms – a camel,' Jacob called after him.

To anyone else, the word *camel* would have produced an expression of bewilderment, for the souk was full of camels – one of them cheerfully chewing at Andy's hair. Only Jack knew exactly what Jacob meant, the camel that had helped and supported him in his quest to find Saleem – his best friend, Bud.

Reluctantly, he retraced his steps. 'But that's impossible! How can anything happen to Bud? He's magical …'

'*Hsst! Hsst!* my Lord Burnside,' Jacob screeched.

Behind them, a party of American tourists had stopped to admire the pottery on the stall. With loud exclamations of joy, they held various pieces up to the light, to examine them more closely. A tall man with a camera, its telephoto lens protruding from his chest like a double cheeseburger, tapped Jacob on the shoulder.

'I say, sir, this pottery – it's from Fes, isn't it?'

Jacob swung round glaring. '*Yes, yes, yes!* From Fes, but it is not for sale.'

'Not for sale?' the tall man repeated, sounding bewildered. 'Why not? Is it all sold?'

'*No, no, no!*' Jacob's hand erupted into the air, like a spinning top. 'Come back tomorrow. It will be for sale then.'

'But I won't be here tomorrow. We're on a tour. Twelve countries in fifteen days,' the man boasted proudly. '*Isn't that right, guys?*' He beamed at the little party standing behind him, his wife's head scarcely visible over the capacious shoulder-bag she was clutching to her chest. 'It's my sons' first visit over here. *Great country.* So, wha'd'ye say? That set of dishes? How much?' The American waved a fistful of notes in the air.

His teenage sons, sporting spots on their faces and blue train-tracks on their teeth, grimaced apologetically at Jack, embarrassed by the fuss their dad was making.

'*Go away, go away, go away!* There is no time for this.' Jacob's second hand joined his first, his fingers behaving more like twittering birds than spinning tops. 'My Lord Burnside, we must talk privately – somewhere quiet …'

'Did he say, *Lord?*' the little woman exclaimed. She gazed at Jack as if she had never before come across a fair-haired boy, wearing a T-shirt, jeans and trainers. 'You're a Lord – *a genu-ine British Lord?*'

'I wish,' Jack said with a grin. 'It's his little joke.'

'Oh, pity.' Baffled, the tourists wandered off, the man glaring indignantly over his shoulder.

'How come Bud is missing?' Jack repeated.

'*My Lord Burnside, this is not the place to bandy secrets,*' Jacob hissed.

'But this is exactly the place.' A blast of bellicose music, accompanied by what sounded like a cat shrieking, thundered out of a pair of speakers, attached to a pole above their heads. 'You could shout all the secrets of the world and nobody would notice.'

'*No, no, no!* You must come with me,' Jacob said, ignoring Jack's remark.

'I told you,' Jack said, determined to stand his ground. 'I can't leave my friends.' Uncomfortably aware of the eyes scrutinising his face, 'There's nothing I can do about it – honest. Can't you make another? I've seen you carve identical wooden camels …'

'If I could make another, do you think I would be standing in a smelly market, bandying words with a boy who has obviously forgotten what loyalty to his friends means. *May the Gods preserve me from such ingratitude.*'

As the sentence spilled into the air, Jacob's voice rose higher and higher, until it soared above the screeching tones of the female pop star, blasting through the speakers. Passers-by stared curiously.

Jack caught at the merchant's sleeve. '*Calm down*,' he muttered embarrassed.

'I say, Jack, is this chap bothering you?' Rob and Andy appeared at his side, their purchases forgotten.

'No, of course not, Rob.' Jack said to the burly defender. 'Er … this is Jacob … er … he works with my dad,' he added, his face flushed and ashamed, vividly recalling how on more than one occasion Bud had saved his life. 'He was telling me about the problems they're having building the refinery.'

'It didn't sound like that,' said Andy, a worried frown on his face.

Jack stepped away from the stall out of earshot, pulling his friends with him. 'I haven't seen Dad for ages so I want to have a chat with Jacob. Cover for me, will you?'

The two boys eyed Jacob doubtfully.

'Are you sure? He looks kind of weird.'

'And Barney said …'

'I know, Andy.' Jack made an effort to smile. 'But this is different. I really need to talk to him. I promise I'll stay here.'

'But what if you vanish and end up a white slave?'

'That's not likely to happen, Rob,' Jack said, adding a nervous, *unless I can't help it*, under his breath.

Rob pulled a face. 'OK. Ten minutes then. But I don't like it.'

'I'm sorry, Jacob.' Jack crossed the narrow walkway back to the little stall. '*That was stupid of me.*'

'No matter, my Lord, you are here now.'

Bowing, the sorcerer ushered Jack inside the little stall and gestured to him to sit, as if he was a guest of great importance.

The pottery stall was no different from a hundred others Jack had already seen in the market. A fold-up trestle table substituted for a counter, covered by an ornate tablecloth to protect the fine glaze on the pottery. Nests of bowls were on display, the pieces stacking neatly one into another, reminding Jack of their meal the previous night. The waiter at the hotel had explained that Meza was the traditional way of starting a meal; a dozen or so little dishes all different, among them yoghurt with cucumber, miniature kebabs and humous – served with pita bread, wrapped in a linen napkin to keep it hot. At the hotel the bowls had been plain white. Here, the dishes had been fired to a fine glaze so as to be almost transparent, shot through with blues and green like water.

Protected by the counter, the barrage of noise diminished into the background; the light softening, becoming shadowy as if they had entered a cave.

'Tea, my Lord.' Jacob picked up a small glass urn, overlaid with silver filigree.

A carpet had been laid on the ground behind the little counter. Nodding his thanks, Jack sat down tucking his feet under him. 'But make it quick, Jacob, I can't stay long. So what is the problem?'

With yet another of those bone-crunching glances, which made Jack feel like a worm, Jacob inched himself laboriously into a cross-legged position.

'A great evil has overtaken our land, my Lord.'

'But you said everything was fine,' Jack protested. 'Anyway, I'm not bothered about your great evil – I came here to ask about Bud, remember.'

Jacob tipped some lumps of brown sugar into a small pot, offering them to Jack. 'It is the same, my Lord Burnside. But you are quite correct. The kingdom – remains quite safe. It is beyond the kingdom where people dwell in fear. Yet, no one will speak of it. They stay locked in their own homes, leaving their crops untended. In one village men threw stones.' Jacob sipped at his tea, his hooded-eyes careworn. 'That is not the behaviour of the inhabitants of our land. We are a friendly people.

'I travelled across the mountain road towards Pulah, in the northwest, hoping to discover more. But no sooner had I set my foot on that pathway when my vision began to fade, until I could see no more than a few feet in front of me. It was as if something had blocked my path, an impenetrable shield – I could neither approach nor pass through.'

'Like a fog, you mean, a thick white cloud?' Jack suggested, intrigued.

'Not white – definitely not white. This is more …' Jacob covered his face with his hands. 'When you cover your eyes there is only darkness.'

Jack copied his gesture. 'So?'

'There could only be one explanation; a sorcerer lived in those mountains with an aura of such intense evil that no light could penetrate it.' Jacob's fingers plucked at the fabric of his gown, expressing his extreme agitation.

Jack groaned. Extracting information from Jacob was like buying a magazine, with an exciting story lurking somewhere in its pages. Only problem was, you had to wade through all twenty-six issues to find it.

'But what have ignorant peasants, frightened of everything, got to do with a black curtain in the mountains? They don't live anywhere near the mountains, do they?'

'*I have told you, I cannot yet determine what is troubling the people of our land,*' Jacob's hands flew into the air. 'But to come across such a phenomenon is alarming in itself.'

'And what do you mean by aura?'

'All sorcerers are surrounded by an aura.'

'Even you, Jacob?'

'*Hsst! Hsst!*' The sorcerer glared. 'It is like a circle, radiating out in every direction; the greater the power the greater the aura. For sorcerers that follow the light, the aura is warm and welcoming, rather like a wall of thick air. As you travel through it, it bends round you allowing you to pass. For sorcerers that follow the dark, the aura is solid – difficult to pass through.'

'OK, so let me get my head round this,' Jack said slowly. Jacob's explanation reminded him of an algebra lesson, you needed to hear it at least twice before it made sense. 'What you're saying is … a powerful sorcerer lives in the mountains … and he's evil … because … because …' Jacob's hands fluttered, as if seeking to pluck the words from Jack's mouth. 'His aura is black.'

Jacob nodded.

'And you believe – whoever it is – is doing something so scary … no one dares talk about it,' Jack ended the sentence in a rush.

'That's it, exactly, my Lord Burnside,' Jacob beamed triumphantly. 'Have some more tea.'

'I haven't drunk this yet, Jacob.'

It was all very well Jacob saying, *that's it exactly*, but with Jacob nothing was ever exact, it always had more twists than a corkscrew.

'I still don't understand why Bud is missing? What's he got to do with it?' Jack said. The sorcerer's hands ran up the opposite sleeve of his gown like rabbits being chased by a fox. 'You don't mean to tell me you sent Bud to discover what is going on?'

Jacob shrugged, his hands lifting into the air as if explaining to his gods that it really wasn't his fault. 'But of course. With his magical powers, such an aura cannot affect him.'

'Then why hasn't he returned?'

Jacob shook his head mournfully. 'I believe it is this danger, which also brings fear to our land, that binds him.'

'But why?' Jack blew on his tea to cool it. 'I mean – perhaps he was blown-up or caught in a volcano or something.'

'My Lord Burnside, you of all people are aware that for the camel, his only enemy is light.'

'That's true.'

Lying against a leg of the trestle table was a large canvas bag, the half-finished carving of a donkey on the ground. Jacob frequently earned his living carving wooden animals but, as far as Jack was aware, only one had the power to move through time and space, dissolving back into its wooden form when the sun rose.

'So how are you going to get him back?' he said, beginning to appreciate Jacob's concern. He bobbed up to show Andy and Rob he was still there and hadn't been spirited away, immediately sitting down again.

Jacob beamed. 'You will go.'

For a moment Jack thought he'd misheard. '*Me!*' he gasped.

Jacob leaned forward gazing intently at the boy, sitting opposite him under the canvas awning, his eyes glittering under their lids.

'I told you, *I can't* – even if I wanted to,' Jack protested strenuously. 'I'm on a *supervised* football tour with fourteen other boys. Do you understand what that means, Jacob? I have to account for my whereabouts *at all times*. Tomorrow, for instance, there's a match. Friday's a rest day. We play a friendly game Saturday morning, go sightseeing as a group on Saturday afternoon and Sunday ... there's a match Monday evening and we fly back first thing Tuesday,' he gasped for breath. 'I'm really sorry; I'd liked to have helped ...'

The memory of saying those exact same words once before came flashing back. Jack swallowed loudly. Last time they'd landed him in a heap of trouble.

He shook his head, adding forcefully, '*But this time it really is impossible.*'

Jacob's hand did a little dance in the air. 'It will all be arranged, you will see. We will meet the day after tomorrow. Take a taxi to the

Jellalabar Road. It lies outside the city on the route to Fes and is visited by many of the tourists, who wish to buy the fine pottery of the region. Ask for the pottery market. I will be waiting for you.'

Catching sight of the time Jack leapt to his feet, his head brushing against the fabric of the awning. Jeez! They'd be late for the coach if they didn't get a move on.

'I must go. Thanks for the tea.' Jacob hadn't listened to one word he'd said. *It was totally impossible.* Hadn't he made that clear?

Jacob rose quickly to his feet thrusting a small tin into Jack's hands. 'Some sweets, my Lord?'

'Fabulous, Jacob!' Jack flashed him a guilty smile. 'And I'm really, very sorry! I'm sure he'll turn up sooner or later.'

He crossed the few metres of path to where Rob and Andy were impatiently waiting, wearing their brand new watches. Looking back, Jack saw Jacob brush the tips of his fingers against his forehead in a traditional salaam. His head swirled.

'Jack, where on earth did ye meet that weirdo? My dad'ud not let me within a mile of anyone like that,' Andy jumped on him as soon they were out of earshot.

'Oh, come on, Andy, he's not that bad. He's – what you call – eccentric.'

'*Eccentric!* That's putting it mildly.' Rob rebuked. 'Half the time it sounded as if you were having a fight to the death.'

'Yeah, but he makes great sweets. Here, have one.'

Jack opened the box of honey sweetmeats. Feeling desperately miserable, he handed the box to his friends hoping it would stop their nagging. Somehow, he had to see Jacob again – if only to convince him that any plan to search for Bud would not include him. Behind them, a crowd of German tourists trailed along the crowded pathways, the eccentric figure no longer visible.

Chapter Four

An Illegal Tackle

'Right lads you have two choices. *Either* you can let these boys beat you and ruin the rest of your visit here – wishing you'd done this or that differently, and scored enough goals to win – *or* you can go back out there and beat the crap out of them. So what'll it be!'

Eleven voices shouted back. 'BEAT THEM.'

'Then stop pussy-footing around,' Barney said. 'You're fitter, better trained and they're keeping you off the ball and stealing all the chances. And when you do get a shot, what do you do, eh Burnside?'

'Balloon it over the goalmouth,' said Jack bitterly.

'Exactly! You're lucky, the way you were playing, it's only *one goal* they scored and you haven't got a dozen or more to claw back in the second half. So this is *make your mind up time*, lads. Did we come here to lose?'

'NO!' roared the team.

'SO WHAT ARE YOU GOING TO DO?'

'WIN!'

'You bet'cha sweet life you are, lads, so go out there and make it happen.'

Pumped up and determined, the team clattered back out of the changing room and onto the pitch; floodlit and with a vociferous local crowd backing the home team – a few English tourists, from their hotel, forlornly cheering their poor first-half showing. Their saviour had been Andy, in goal, aided and abetted by some able defending by Rob – cheerfully substituting for Syd, who had picked up a tummy bug.

26

The team doctor, after visiting the patient, had called the boys together, advising them that buying kebabs from a stall at the roadside was definitely, *"not one of the must things to do when visiting the Middle East."* Since then, Syd hadn't stirred from his room, boasting to his mates that he could reach the loo in under three seconds, even from the balcony.

Jack studied the field. Now it was the turn of the midfield and strikers to show what they could do. The whistle sounded for the second half, *and with* only *thirty minutes to do it.* If they were going to score it was up to him since Marco, in left field, was closely marked. He'd created their only opportunity in the first half, and now a tight defence was keeping him firmly corralled.

Jack had been astonished how well the twelve-year-old played. Of course, having a birthday in January was always an advantage in junior football. Still, he had fitted in well with their team and had definitely made an impression, creating gaps where none existed.

A loose ball came bouncing over the turf towards him. Flashing a friendly smile at the boy shadowing him, Jack picked it up and, easily dodging his opponent, raced up into the top third of the pitch. Beyond him the goalmouth was beginning to crowd up. With Marco unable to break free, Bram, Tyrone and Gary were jockeying for position – but there was a gap, since everyone was expecting the attack to come from Marco and had grouped themselves accordingly.

Hooking the ball, Jack made it dance in the air, hunting for someone unmarked to take the cross. Tyrone, outsmarting his opponent, darted into position, signalling he was ready. Jack hesitated. The gap was still there, not big but tantalising – like an advertisement on a giant hoarding – drawing him in until he daren't ignore it any longer. Grabbing a few more yards, he ducked and weaved as players poured towards him. *Could he?* Applying spin to the ball, he watched it swerve in the air and thunder into the net.

'That'll show 'em,' he muttered. Bram jumped high up on his shoulders with excitement, two others hugging him. Jack glanced over to where Barney was sitting, a big grin on his face. Two minutes into the second half and they were all square.

The tension mounted as minutes ticked by and the scores remained equal. Jack felt like a cornered rat, impeded at every step by his opposite number, clinging like a leech, his right foot constantly poised to tackle. Even the crowd were focussing their attention on him – concerned that he might attempt something equally daring.

Play ebbed and flowed up and down the pitch, like the tide at the seaside, the crowd roaring each time the Rabat team besieged Andy in goal. But Andy had also listened to their coach at half-time. Flinging himself diagonally across the ground, arms and legs akimbo, he reached out with his fingertips, and the crowd groaned its disappointment.

Jack raced off down the pitch, his shadow in hot pursuit. Ten minutes to go. They had to make a chance. He sped up, indicating to Tim he wanted the pass. It roared in from centre midfield. Collecting it with his right boot, he accelerated.

From behind a leg scythed across his foot, jerking the ball away from his control and over the line. Instantly the referee's whistle sounded, Jack spinning round to face him and argue his case if necessary. There was no need, the referee had clearly seen the illegal tackle. Tim ran up to take the corner, while Jack and – what seemed like – a thousand others jockeyed for position. The ball came in, high and wide.

Almost a head taller than the boys scuffling for possession below him, Jack made contact with the ball, striking it firmly. He watched unbelieving as the goalkeeper – anticipating the direction of his header – dived to his right and got his fingers to it. A defender, backing him up, moved to clear it and the crowd roared its relief.

Then the ball twisted against a stud on the defender's boot and ricocheted back across the line.

IT WAS IN. OWN GOAL OR NOT. IT WAS IN!

Hardly believing his luck, Jack spun round to celebrate his second goal and cannoned into his shadow. He stepped back, his hand automatically stretching out to touch the boy's arm in a friendly apology. Next moment, his leg was hooked from under him and he fell sprawling to the ground, where he lay spread-eagled and helpless. For a second or two no one noticed, the referee sorting a carefully-orchestrated melee of players protesting the goal. Then Jack heard the whistle sound angrily. The referee ran over waving the English coach onto the pitch.

As Barney ran up, the referee began jabbering angrily at the player who seemed the most likely candidate for Jack's sudden appearance flat on the ground, his hand already reaching into his pocket for a red card.

'Jack, how bad are you hurt?'

'I'm OK, Barney, but it's twisted,' he muttered, the pain making him gasp.

'Stay still, lad. I'll get your boot off. Worth it though!'

'You bet,' said Jack, grinning despite the pain soaring through him. 'But I can't play on.'

'Don't worry about it, you've made Leonard's day.' Barney cut the laces with his penknife, carefully sliding the boot off. Jack grimaced, his foot already beginning to swell. 'He's already decided he'll make the team Saturday and has a big grin on his face.'

He beckoned a couple of burly helpers onto the pitch and, demonstrating how to make a chair using crossed hands, helped Jack up.

The crowd broke into a half-hearted cheer of sympathy, secretly cursing Jack for his goal and glad to be seeing the back of him.

'Can we hold on?' Jack said, looping his arms round the men's shoulders.

'You bet.' Barney, carrying Jack's damaged boot dangling from one finger, brought up the rear. 'Your team mates won't let you down, I promise.'

'OK, Coach. But there's no need for you to stay. I've seen it all before, so I know the drill.' The referee's whistle sounded to recommence play. *Five minutes plus injury time.* Well, it was up to his team-mates. Nothing further he could do to influence the result.

It was enough. Ten minutes later a jubilant team surged down into the dressing room. They crowded through into the treatment room to congratulate a grinning Jack, his foot covered with an ice pack, to help the pain and swelling, and already feeling a lot better.

'OK, lads, enough's enough,' said Barney, wading into the noisy group. 'Hurry up and get changed. You've got a reception with the home team, and the mayor and suchlike. Jack? Sorry lad, you're grounded, got to stay off that foot.'

'Can't I use crutches, Barney? There's some here.'

'You're not going anywhere today. Perhaps tomorrow, if the swelling goes down, but my guess is it'll be worse tomorrow. And don't expect to get a boot on in under a week.'

'Tough luck, Jack.' Sympathetic hands patted him on the back, as one by one the boys drifted off to get changed.

'Mr Woods will escort you back to the hotel,' Barney said. 'I've got a taxi waiting.'

'But I'm not changed,' Jack protested, annoyed at being railroaded just when he wanted to bask in the glory of his two goals.

'You can change straight into your pyjamas and watch TV, OK?'

Tim's dad, who had travelled with the team to Morocco, collected Jack's bag, carrying it out to the taxi. The streets were busy with bright lights everywhere. Full of shoppers, a constant stream of cars hampered their taxi driver's determination to drive at breakneck speed. Frustrated, he careered headlong into the car in front, jamming on his brakes in time to avert a crash, loudly cursing and thumping the horn.

Jack saw and heard nothing. Resting his foot on the seat beside him, he stared defiantly out of the window, a storm of thoughts invading his head. With his bad foot, he would definitely be confined to the hotel. But how could Jacob have known?

'Oh – er,' he groaned aloud. Jacob expected him to appear in the morning. And he'd only gone and forgotten where.

'Your foot aching, Jack?' Mr Woods patted him on the shoulder. 'I'm not surprised with this maniac at the wheel.'

The taxi slammed to a halt outside the hotel. Casting a grateful glance at its solid edifice, Mr Woods scrambled out. Paying the driver, he hurried up the steps into the foyer, leaving Jack to follow more slowly on his crutches.

The vast circular lobby, with its sweeping counters, was bustling. Set amidst elegant marble walls and delicately patterned archways, groups of guests milled about eagerly discussing where to go for dinner. An immensely-tall individual, dressed as a Bedouin, circled the lobby with a tray of small glasses and a brass and glass urn, offering tea to anyone standing in one spot for more than a second or two.

Jack's leg was already beginning to throb again, and he reluctantly realised that Barney was right – as usual. He hopped slowly across the lobby to fetch his key.

'Football?' The desk clerk smiled sympathetically.

'Yeah!' Jack pulled a face. 'Seven-four-six, please.'

'Scored the winning goal, though.' Mr Woods patted Jack on the back. 'Get him something nice for his supper, he deserves it. I've sent your bag up to your room, Jack. Will you be all right if I leave now?' he said, anxious to join his son and the other members of the team at the reception.

'I'm fine, honest.'

'Right!' Mr Woods set off across the lobby. 'See you in the morning then, and stay off that foot,' he called loudly.

Jack glowered at the gossiping people, the sound of laughter constantly ringing out. It was so unfair. Everyone in the world was having fun except him.

'Would you like me to take your order, sir?' the receptionist said, his bright voice trained to sound cheery whatever the occasion.

'Yes, please,' Jack dredged up a grin, instantly feeling more positive at the thought of food. 'I'm starving. Could I have a double cheeseburger with chips?'

'Of course, sir. And to follow?'

'Ice Cream, please.'

'Which flavour, sir?'

'Chocolate and vanilla. Can I have some of each?' The man nodded. 'And I s'pose you don't have those little cakes … the ones with nuts and honey in that pastry?'

'Baclava?' The clerk scribbled on a pad. He picked up the phone and dialled room service.

Jack eyes wandered round the vast atrium, with its domed roof of blues and golds, wishing he had paid more attention to what Jacob was saying. 'Excuse me … is there a pottery market near here?'

The clerk paused, his hand over the receiver. 'Pottery market? Never heard of one, sir.' He turned away, speaking into the phone.

A woman's voice broke in. 'I couldn't help overhearing. There's a market on the Jellalabar Road. We went there today.'

Jack swivelled awkwardly on his crutches.

A middle-aged man and woman stood behind him, patiently waiting to collect their key. The man's face was scarlet with heat and sun after a day's sight-seeing, and his wife was using her hat to fan him.

'Jellalabar Road, *that's right*!' Jack exclaimed, his eyes shining with excitement. 'Great! You went today? So how can I get there?'

The woman laughed. 'Not on that foot, dear,' she said in a motherly tone of voice. 'It's out in the desert, on the road to Fes. But when your foot is better, you can take a taxi.'

Jack grinned his thanks and hobbled over towards the lift, several guests idly following his progress. Suddenly, his smile flashed off replaced by a loud and audible groan. The attendant, about to press the button for the seventh floor, looked up startled.

'Sorry,' Jack indicated his foot. 'It hurts.'

The lift shot upwards.

If only it had been his foot. But it wasn't. Andy and Rob would have to be told and Jack already knew they wouldn't like it – they'd made that crystal clear – which meant he'd owe them big time.

* * *

By Friday morning Jack's foot had swollen up like a balloon. The team doctor instantly recommended complete rest and constant ice packs. Jack seesawed between total pain-filled misery, frustration at being left behind while the team were out having fun, and determination to carry out his plan.

Eventually, he decided that pretending to argue and sound really upset was the best way to guarantee being confined to his room. Barney would never allow member of the team to best him, no matter how good an argument he put up.

'You will remain here and the doctor will see you again on Monday. Meanwhile, have a holiday,' he said, glaring at the invalid.

'OK, Coach, that's exactly what I will do – thanks,' retorted Jack glumly, his expression changing to one of triumph the moment the door closed behind Barney and the doctor.

'Right, you two, you heard what our coach said. I'm to have a holiday. So I'm having a holiday – only thing is, not in this hotel. I'm off to visit my dad.' Having started the lie, there seemed little Jack could do but embellish it and make it sound truthful. 'It's absolute ages since I saw him and he won't be back in England for months yet. I can be there and back in a couple of days.'

'*You're crazy!*' stormed Rob. 'I can't see Barney letting you go anywhere on your own. And don't say you're not on your own. If you're with that weirdo, however hard you try to make him believe your dad's at the end of the line, he'll lock you up first.'

'I'm not going to tell him.'

'*You're mad, Jack*, if ye get caught ...' began Andy.

'I won't get caught, not if you cover for me. Come on, there's nothing to it,' Jack added, noting the mutinous expression on Andy's face. If only he could confide in his friends, it would be like taking out insurance in case he didn't reappear. 'You could hide an army in the reception hall alone. And if I'm confined to the hotel and anyone asks, I can always be watching telly in the lounge or sitting by the swimming pool. It'ud take days to search this place.'

'What about'ye meals?' Andy said.

'You can eat them.'

'*But if they find out?*' Rob groaned, tugging at his hair.

'They won't,' said Jack firmly, far more firmly than he was actually feeling. 'And if they do, you plead ignorance. After all, what can they do? Send me home? We leave Tuesday morning anyway.'

'No, but they can stop you playing for the team.' Rob sighed miserably.

'Oh cheer up, Rob, I'd do it for you.'

Rob and Andy exchanged looks. 'OK, we promise. But you'll be back.'

'Absolutely,' Jack said – the fingers on both hands well and truly crossed.

Chapter Five

The Jellalabar Road

Jack waited patiently, sitting quietly in his room until the team had left the hotel. Once the coast was clear, he took the lift to the lower-ground floor to avoid being spotted by the clerks in reception, or any of the dozens of porters that ran up and down the foyer ordering taxis and running errands for guests. The lift jerked to a standstill, the gate slid back and he hobbled out.

The team had already explored the lower level where the swimming pool and sun terraces were situated. It was early and the terraces remained deserted, except for a maid carefully sweeping up the debris from the day before. Early risers, eager to explore, had already departed for a full day of sightseeing. Only the idle few were still thinking about breakfast, to be followed by a spot of April sunshine, and bright beach towels already littered the sun-beds scattered round the pool.

Beyond the terraces, the grounds fell away to form landscaped gardens, bright with colour from exotic plants and ferns. But Jack wasn't interested in sun terraces or gardens. On this level, there was something much more important – a small gate that opened in one direction only, outwards into the street. Pushing it open, he hailed a taxi. As they swept past the hotel entrance, with its polished marble columns and half-circle of national flags fluttering in the breeze, Jack ducked down pretending to tie his trainers, in case anyone that knew him was hanging about.

The ramshackle old vehicle, its gears grinding ferociously, headed out through the city and, for a time, Jack could have sworn they were driving round in circles. Eventually the centre, with its shops and offices, was left behind and they dived into a massive construction site of high-rise apartment blocks. Some were recently completed, others simply a concrete shell like a thousand empty eyes peering down. The site was ringed by billboards covered in Arabic writing, with pictures of men advertising deodorants, aftershave and televisions; the sandy-coloured wasteland criss-crossed by newly-laid tarmac roads, dissected at intervals by large traffic islands.

Traffic was thick and his driver dealt with it contemptuously, using his brakes and horn with equal abandon. Clearing the city, they headed out into the suburbs where the high-rises ended and the villas with gardens began. Gradually, the tarmac road petered out and the driver eased his foot off the accelerator as his tyres hit a dirt track. They weren't alone. A convoy of taxis converged behind them on the dusty road. This comforted Jack no end, his mind heaving with visions of what might happen to him in a strange land, and in a strange taxi.

Soon a clutter of tents appeared heralding the market and the taxi slowed. The long parade of vehicles swooped past, parking in a neat line next to a dried-up flowerbed, full of grey spiky cactus and palm trees, with bedraggled yellowish-green leaves.

Close by, a sign in Arabic and English had been tacked to a post hammered into the sun-baked ground. Advertising a pottery exhibition, an arrow pointed to a string of single-story buildings. Constructed from breezeblocks roughly sandwiched together, splodges of grey cement bulged from the cracks, like a jam sandwich with too much jam on it. Behind them was a decrepit-looking café, its roof of dried palm-leaves drooping down over the tables in one corner. An elderly waiter wandered about tidying chairs and mopping the metal tables with a wet cloth. A stray gust of wind blew grains of sand into the air. They settled on the tables he had just cleaned and, half-heartedly, he flicked his cloth at them.

'You know where I stop?' The driver stared pointedly at Jack's crutches.

A few tourists were already wandering about, lingering by the stalls and blocking Jack's view. Anxiously, he cast an eye over the sea of canvas on the far side of the track, hoping he hadn't come all this way on a wild-goose chase. Most of the tents were old and tattered, only a few having sparkling-white guy ropes and canvas free from water stains. Rickety wooden-tables served as counters; the vendors, in their traditional white dress, sipping cups of Arabic coffee while they waited for customers to arrive.

Jack caught a glimpse of a tent standing on its own, away from the hubbub of the market; a camel and a donkey, tethered side by side, attached to a post nearby.

'This'll do,' he said, instinct telling him he had arrived.

The driver leant back to open the door. Jack stuffed some money into his hands and stepped out, making sure to place his good foot down first. Taking the weight on his crutches, he hopped on to the dirt track watching the taxi disappear back the way it had come.

* * *

The tent resembled a motley collection of old clothes, roughly tacked together. Originally striped, the harsh climate had bleached them until they blended well with the brownish-green scrub. Abruptly, the flap of the tent was pushed aside, a familiar figure standing in the doorway.

'My Lord Burnside.' Jacob sidled out of the opening, his hands already twisting and turning in their familiar pattern. 'It is good.'

'How did you know I'd be here? I only knew it myself last night.'

Jacob's shoulders and arms rose into the air. 'Once you had decided that you could not let that curs-ed animal fall into harm, I knew you would not sleep until you had found a way.'

Jack followed him through the entrance, his eyes rapidly adjusting to the shadows cast by the sun beating against its fabric walls.

'Sit, sit, sit!' Jacob extended a welcoming hand towards a collection of cushions on the carpeted ground.

'Jacob – it's not like that,' Jack protested miserably. This was the worst ever, Jacob being nice. It was all wrong.

Jacob examined the boy intently, his eyes glinting sharply – his hands and arms silent.

'Then tell me what it is like, my Lord Burnside.'

'I didn't exactly come to rescue Bud,' Jack admitted, feeling ashamed. 'So don't go thinking I did. It's more like … well …er …' Anxious to have his confession over and done, the words flew out. 'I need to get my foot better so I can play in the match on Monday and …' he paused. 'I *hoped* you could mend it,' he added more slowly, his voice scarcely audible.

It was a relief to get it off his chest, but he still felt wretched. 'The thing is …' Jack drew himself to his full height, hoping to cut a more imposing figure, in spite of his crutches. The previous night in bed, he had rehearsed and rehearsed his speech, repeating the words time and time again, to make sure he didn't forget them.

'Last time – everything was so scary. I was left on my own in the palace – finding out stuff as I went along. This time, before I even think about agreeing, you've got to tell me everything. I can't help, *and I won't help*, unless I know what I'm getting in to. I've grown up a lot and I'm not the gullible fool I was the last time we met.'

'No, my Lord, you have indeed learned much but there is much to learn.'

'So you'll tell me?'

'As you will. But you will eat first?'

'Yes! Absolutely,' Jack said. 'I'm starving.'

'In that, I hope your appetite has not grown in step with your body. For if it has, there will not be sufficient food in this country.'

Jack laughed, all at once feeling much more cheerful. 'Jacob, *you actually told a joke!* I wish Bud had been here, he'd have fainted.' He sat himself down on the cushions, his crutches on the ground beside him.

A small fire was burning at the back of the tent. Removing a long skewer, on which pieces of lamb had been grilling, Jacob settled a brass water pot on the glowing embers. Then, filling a small dish with rice added the meat. Offering the dish to Jack, he returned to his seat against a bank of cushions.

'So why is finding Bud so important?'

Jacob was silent for a moment or two, as if struggling to hold on to his secrets. 'Because his magic is special and cannot be replicated.'

Jack's paused, his fingers full of food. 'I said *everything*, Jacob.'

'But you cannot understand everything, my Lord Burnside,' the sorcerer protested. Noticing Jack's stubborn expression, he bowed his head and began to speak.

'The greatest of all sorcerers, who lived a thousand years or more ago, foretold a future of unending battles between good and evil. To prevent this warring, he traded a portion of his own power to create a being.'

Outside the tent came the constant swish of tyres; car doors slamming as taxis, jammed with eager tourists, started to arrive. Now, on the other side of the canvas wall there would be dust and haggling, money passing from hand to hand in exchange for fine pottery. Tourists laughing and joking, completely unaware of the secrets being whispered not twenty metres from them.

'Not a human being – subject to life and death – simply a being, whose power can only be harnessed by those that follow the light – a familiar.'

Jack groaned silently. Jacob was quite right; it was useless asking him to explain things – the more he explained, the more confusing everything got.

'What's a familiar?'

'A talisman – a companion, if that is easier to understand; one who helps on their journey and battles with them against evil.'

'And is Bud like that?' Jack paused his chewing to ask.

'That camel! *The plague of my life!*' Jacob's hands rent the air. 'Foul, bad-tempered and argumentative. And you ask if that is my familiar? How can that be? How can a bovine eater of hay be my guide?' His voice spiralled upwards following his restless arms high into the air. 'Not content with simply becoming an affliction, like some rare disease, he disappears – and this plagues me even more, because now I have to risk life and limb to rescue him.'

'So if Bud isn't your familiar – what is he?' Jack said, ignoring the sorcerer's ranting.

'Do I have to tell you every single detail? At this rate two days will have passed before we leave this tent,' railed Jacob, his outburst breaking the tension.

'Two days?'

'Is it not Sunday when you told your friends you will return?' the sorcerer said, his voice quite calm again.

Jack grimaced at being reminded of the lies he had told. 'Go on.'

Jacob got to his feet. Removing the bubbling water from the fire, he poured it into the little glass and silver urn. 'The camel is simply a wooden statue that I carved when I was boy, to whom the skills of a familiar have been given.'

'So why can't these sorcerers with the black aura do that, create a thingamajig – *you know* – a familiar?'

'Because such men are also greedy, incapable of parting with sufficient power to create such a being. Instead, they devote their minds solely to the acquisition of power; gaining it by trickery and deception, if all else fails.'

'OK, I understand *why* you need to recover him, but you still haven't said how you plan to do it.'

'We must go and seek him. As you draw nearer, your friendship for the beast will create a fusion between you and you will begin to sense his presence. 'Tea?'

'That was scrummy, thank you.' Jack handed back his empty dish. Jacob reminded him of the pottery being sold in the market; something extraordinary wrapped in layers of old newspaper and shoved into a tacky plastic carrier. 'OK, I can do that. But we're hundreds of miles away and we've not got long.'

'That is not your concern, my Lord Burnside. I will get you to the mountains, and you will find the animal.' Jacob sat down again, placing the tea tray on the ground beside him.

'*Me? I'm not doing this alone,*' Jack shouted wildly. '*I told you – not again and especially not without Bud.*'

'But how can I go?' Jacob wailed. His arms flew into the air, knocking against the silver tea urn. It rocked unsteadily and a stream of scalding liquid spurted out. '*You tell me! You tell me!* Have I not already explained to you that a sorcerer is surrounded by an aura of power? If I attempt to enter the kingdom of Mendorun …'

'*Who?*' Forgetting, Jack made to leap to his feet. He yelped with pain, falling back down again. When he could speak, 'You mean *that* Mendorun – Saladin's friend? The man that read my mind?'

He shuddered, remembering Mendorun's eyes powering through the spectators at the football match seeking him out, reading his thoughts as easily as a book.

'Sorry, but that changes everything. I'm not going anywhere near him. Besides, what if Saladin's about? He wants to kill me, remember?'

'That cannot be, my Lord, that cur will be long gone.'

'Well, I'm not chancing it. Not even my leg's worth that. You'll have to find someone else or go yourself,' Jack said in a determined voice.

Jacob's hands began to revolve around one another, rivalling the rotor blades on a helicopter and, at such a speed, Jack wondered if like them he was about to take off. He caught the words, *"pestilential boy,"* among Jacob's unintelligible mutterings.

'Did I not explain why it is impossible for me to set foot on that mountain? I might as well announce my arrival by ringing his front door bell. No! Your only thought is of your safety. Will I not give you my other camel, who can infiltrate the darkness without anyone becoming aware? Will I not make sure that nothing evil happens to you? *And will I not return you safely to your hotel in time to play the match on Monday?'*

Jack sat frozen to the spot, as Jacob's wild tirade blasted his ears.

'But I can't play on Monday, Jacob, I've got an injured foot,' he ventured, hoping to stem the noise.

'Forgive me, my Lord Burnside, I forgot your foot,' said Jacob instantly solicitous, his anger vanished. 'That is easily dealt with and then we will go – no?'

Jack sighed loudly. 'OK, I give in. But you've got to promise I'll be safe.'

'My Lord, as far as I am able I do say so, for I have seen into the future and you are there. Now, your foot. Place it on the ground.'

'I can't, it hurts.'

'*I did not ask you to walk, simply to put it on the ground,'* Jacob chided. 'Is this to be the pattern of our relationship that you argue every time I ask the simplest thing of you? In which case, I shall be most grateful to receive the pestilential camel's mutterings in exchange for your absence.'

Jack, his face tight and stiff with the tension of Jacob's revelations, broke into a laugh. Quickly untying the bandages on his left foot, he rested it gingerly on the ground.

Jacob took a small box from his sleeve, its lid encrusted with precious stones. Shafts of light, like the points of a star, circled round the gold casket creating a wide halo. Even though Jack had seen the box before, it remained a mystery how something so small could possibly contain enough magic to disappear a whole army of fighting men. But it did, he had seen it happen.

Jacob raised the box into the air, his hands once again steady and strong and, opening the lid, blew very softly across its mouth. A coil of smoke emerged, as if invisible fingers were hauling it up on a gossamer thread. For a moment, it hung motionless in the air like a thick length of rope. Then, snakelike, it slithered down towards the bare foot stretched out on the floor. Alarmed, Jack's drew his foot back.

Jacob's eyes pierced the gloom. 'Be still,' he hissed.

The command, uttered in a voice so unlike Jacob's whinging tone, froze Jack's foot to the spot. As the smoke reached it, coil after coil wound itself round, until there was nothing to be seen except a length of rope, with a leg sticking out of one end. Tentatively, at first, a tingle of warmth struck his toes. Gradually, it spread throughout the entire foot, the heat penetrating the muscles and sinews, travelling up towards his ankle. The warmth intensified, becoming hotter and hotter, until it was almost unbearable. Jack clenched his fists to stop himself crying out, convinced he was being burned alive.

A wind struck, tugging fiercely at his arms and head, and tearing at the fabric of his jeans and shirt. Ignoring the canvas sides of the tent, it lifted his crutches into the air and flung them against the table. Ripping away the rope that held his foot, it banished the heat as if it had never been, the air once again unmoving.

Jack looked down at his foot. It was still there and it felt exactly like the other one. And it wasn't hot any longer. He wriggled his toes – no pain. He wriggled his ankle – not a twinge. Finally, he stood up.

'It doesn't hurt,' he exclaimed.

'No, of course not,' replied Jacob, packing the pots and pans he had used to cook their meal into a saddlebag. 'It is better. Now we go.'

Chapter Six

The Invisible Cave

Jack, in the tunic and head-wrap of a typical street boy, his jeans, shirt and trainers packed in one of the saddlebags, rode with Jacob – the heavily-laden donkey trotting behind.

'Where are we going?' he said.

'We go to a cave in the mountains, my Lord. From there we will begin our journey.'

'To Sudana?'

'Do you always ask so many questions?'

'Yes. My mother says it's the sign of an active mind.' Jack grinned to himself, constantly wriggling his injured foot, hardly able to believe it no longer hurt. He'd be fit for the match on Monday after all – *provided he got back in time.* Doubt crept into his mind, destroying the happy feeling.

'What if we don't locate Bud straight away?'

'We will keep looking, my Lord.'

'Jeez! I've only got till Sunday, what do we do then?'

Jacob didn't reply and they continued their journey in silence, the splay feet of the camel making no sound on the dusty sand. Only the clicking of the reins, driving the camel towards the distant hills, broke the silence of the clear air.

It was several hours later before the monotony of the dirt track ended, the dry scrub giving way to rocky outcrops on which nothing grew. Jack, lulled into a doze by the gentle swaying of the camel, opened his eyes as the sun slid behind a mountain peak, dimming the brilliance of the light beating against his lids.

The track grew steeper. The camel slowed, its feet unable to grip the loose shale. Finally, it halted altogether, vociferously hissing its displeasure at the stones cutting its feet. Jacob forced it down to its knees, still bellowing loudly, allowing them to dismount. Then, taking the reins, he hauled the protesting animal onto its feet again, leaving Jack to follow with the donkey.

To one side of them a cliff rose vertically into the sky. The other was a sheer drop, flattening into a gentle slope only as it gained the brush-strewn sand. In the distance, the tents of the pottery traders were still visible; a cloud of dust rising into the air, as yet another vehicle arrived or departed back to the city. Jack, his eyes firmly fixed on the ground, followed the rear of the camel as it swayed gracefully up the path. Now his foot was better, he was determined not ruin his chance of making the team by injuring it again. A sudden jerk on the reins caught him off-balance. He stumbled and his arm shot out to break his fall. He swung round to find the donkey backing away down the slope in a determined manner.

'*Whoa*!' he yelled.

'WHOA …whoa …whoa … whoa,' the mountain boomed back.

Spooked by the noise, the donkey headed down the mountain path, Jack chasing after it. He grabbed the dangling reins and dragged the animal to a halt, his feet sliding raggedly across the loose surface. It brayed loudly and, flinging its head into the air, shied backwards, its hind legs clattering the stones at the edge of precipice.

Jack froze, hardly daring to breathe. Nervously, he reached over and grasped its bridle, directing the donkey's head up the path. Looping the reins over his shoulder, he gave them a gentle tug, hoping to encourage the animal to follow him. The reins grew taut. To his horror the animal had now become wedged across the path, its feet splayed outwards, its knees firmly locked.

Jack groaned. How on earth was he to get it moving again? He knew nothing about donkeys. Impatiently, he yanked on the reins. Nothing happened, except for a loud and very ominous creaking. Startled, he caught sight of the donkey's face. Already long, it had grown dramatically longer; its upper lip curled back over the bit, its teeth and gums emerging in a toothy grimace.

'Oh, for Pete's sake, come on, will you,' Jack shouted, losing his temper. Digging his heels into the path, he hauled on the reins. Next moment, he slammed down onto the path as the donkey, as docile as a well-trained dog, trotted neatly up the slope.

'Jeez! The *stupid* animal,' he gasped, the breath knocked out of him by the force of his tumble.

Rolling over onto his hands and knees, he raised his head from the path to glare at the wretched beast. But it was no longer there. It had vanished, and so had Jacob and the camel.

Bewildered, Jack collapsed back down onto the path and rubbed his back, where he had struck it on the ground. Instantly dismissing his original theory – that they might have been spirited away by Martians – as not very likely, he came to the conclusion it had to be one of Jacob's tricks. But which one?

Shakily climbing back onto his feet, Jack raised his left arm. In slow motion he tested the space, flinching back as a pebble broke away clattering noisily over the cliff edge. He hesitated a moment or two before sliding his right foot forward to join his left, his arm held rigidly in front of him. *Nothing.* A shade more confident, he raised his foot again and, taking the weight on his left side, inched forward. Something hard and jagged struck his hand. Rock! Invisible rock! *So that was it.* Jack let go the breath he'd been holding. OK, invisible rock he could cope with.

With his arm outstretched and level with his shoulder, he walked his fingers, in crab-like movements, across the solid rock wall. All of a sudden, they encountered space. Allowing his head to follow his hands, he bent low letting his torso, his hips, and finally his left foot, step through the gap.

A fire burned in the cave, the camel and donkey munching hay from the nose bag, strung from a nail hammered into the rock. Jacob was busily removing something from one of the saddlebags and didn't notice the boy stumble through the entrance.

Jack crouched by the fire pretending to warm his hands, convinced his face had gone white.

'My Lord Burnside, you must forgive me.' Jacob's tone was solicitous. 'I forgot I had not informed you of the cave's existence. I will make you some tea and afterwards we will finish our journey.'

'That's OK, Jacob,' Jack said, hoping he sounded more cheerful than he felt. 'Think nothing of it. But what now? We're still hundreds of miles away. We'll never make it with *that thing*.' He threw a look of absolute loathing at the donkey.

'How did you travel to this country, my Lord?'

'By air, of course. You mean we're *flying back*?' Jack exclaimed. 'So why have we come here? The airport's in Rabat.'

'I have no need of such modern inventions as the aeroplane. My method of travel is similar – but perhaps a little smaller.' Jacob joined him by the fire, immediately serving Jack with the customary glass of tea. He groped about in his sleeve, pulling out the little jewelled casket.

'You have to be joking!' Jack said, convinced if his face hadn't been white before it would be now. 'You mean the box can fly us to Mersham?'

'Not, Mersham. We will go to Asfah. The town lies only a few kilometres from the mountains, although far enough for Mendorun not to sense my presence,' Jacob added, silencing Jack's interruption with a gesture of his hand.

'Can we go anywhere? The moon, for instance.'

'No. All power has its limitations.' Jacob wrapped his hands round the small glass, fragrant steam drifting into the air. 'Moonlight provides its most powerful expression for sun, the ultimate power, strips away lesser magic.'

'So–o …' Jack paused. His eyes wandered round the cave, its corners shadowy and dark; the heavy body of the camel blocking his view of its depths. 'If we were outside in the sun … it wouldn't work.'

'Exactly, my Lord, like that pernicious beast who turns into a block of wood the moment light hits it.' Jacob shook his head, his arms usually so volatile lying limply in his lap, as depressed as their owner's voice sounded.

'But that's fantastic.'

Jack nibbled one of the little cakes that Jacob always served with tea, feeling the warm sweetness of the juice trickle over his tongue. He smiled. It was going to be all right after all – in fact, better than all right. In a moment, he'd be back in Sudana. And, once it was dark, it would be easy to locate Bud. He'd be back in the hotel by … Jack hesitated calculating the journey from the cave to the pottery market. By Saturday afternoon anyway. And with his foot all mended too. *He might even be allowed to go sight-seeing with the team on Sunday.* Idly, he wondered how the team would fare in the friendly taking place on Saturday morning, and whether Petey had finally decided to get rid of his quiff. According to Tyrone, they had been followed round the market by a man who had wanted to sell them a parrot, swearing it was Petey's long-lost brother.

'You're positive the camel can travel from the town and back in one night.' Jack said. 'I can't keep saying *the camel*, it's got to have a name – Betsy – that'll do – our dog's called Betsy.'

Jacob rose swiftly to his feet, placing the box on the ground. 'Do not be afraid, my Lord Burnside, there is nothing to fear from the magic of the box, it will not harm you.'

Brilliant sparks erupted from its jewel-encrusted lid and flew across the room, making the cave walls glow with a greenish-phosphorescence. Smoke poured into the air, billowing about. As if directed by some unseen force, it gathered itself into some semblance of order spinning round and round, spiralling upwards towards the roof of the cave.

Jack swallowed nervously, wondering if travelling by box was like being in an express lift. You stepped in on one floor and, after a burst of ear-popping, stomach-churning speed, feeling awfully dizzy and sick, you stepped out on another.

Jacob, taking up the bridles of the two animals led them into the maelstrom of smoke, where they instantly disappeared. He held out his hand to Jack and, together, they stepped into the whirlwind.

There was a blinding flash of light, a navy sky splashed with stars and moons, followed by a gold and rose-coloured dawn. The sun came up clearing away the mist which had obscured his vision. As the smoke cleared, the cave once again came into focus.

The camel, together with the donkey, completely unperturbed, was standing aimlessly in the middle of the floor taking no notice of anything – everything exactly as it had been a moment before.

'It didn't work, Jacob,' Jack said, sounding disappointed. The sorcerer bent down disappearing the little box into his sleeve. 'We're still in the cave.'

A shaft of amusement penetrated the hooded lids. 'You have not looked far enough, my Lord Burnside. Step outside.'

Jack hurried over to the cave entrance. In the far distance were the billowing green palms of an oasis, as different from the sand-strewn bushes of the Moroccan dirt road as it was possible to find.

Chapter Seven

Asfah

A bubble of excitement began to build inside Jack, as he helped Jacob set up the stall at the edge of the town.

The slopes of the mountain range had given way to fields, criss-crossed by irrigation ditches and planted with vegetables. Jack recognised the long, leafy stalks belonging to the maize plant. In one of the fields a man was ploughing, using a bullock yoked to a hand-driven plough.

Beyond the shade-giving palms, with their deep pools of fresh water, lay the town itself, a maze of streets radiating from a main square. The narrow alleyways were lined with clay-brick houses, surrounded by a perimeter wall, with flat-roofs and small windows, covered with shutters.

It was all so different from his home in Birmingham. The little stalls sold olives and bread, cheese and goats' milk, pots and pans; everything the town's people might need – except there weren't any people. In the town square, a group of men sat outside the coffee house, playing some sort of game with a dice and counters, and dogs slept in the shade of the boxlike houses.

Puzzled, Jack inspected the empty streets noticing a door open and close, allowing a black-garmented figure to fetch water from the well. Something was missing. With a jolt, Jack realised what – there were no children. He hadn't heard or seen a single child since their arrival. If Asfah was anything like Rabat, there should have been gangs of them roaming the streets, bothering any stranger that came into town. Even the market was empty; not a single child badgering the traders for something to eat. He was the only one there.

All at once, the sidelong glances their arrival had attracted became those of suspicion. No one had spoken to them. In fact, come to think of it, the only voices he had heard were those of the traders drinking tea and chatting; their cooking pots swinging from iron rods hung over a fire. Men that didn't live Asfah, who visited for a day or two to sell their goods. The houses behind them were completely silent, as if deserted. *Something was definitely wrong.*

The bubble of excitement burst with a loud bang, leaving Jack feeling sick and dizzy. He stared at the empty streets, his arms encumbered with the dishes and pots they'd been hoping to sell to the villagers. *He'd only gone and done it again!* Flippin' heck! Boasting to Jacob that he'd grown up, and was no longer the gullible fool he'd been before. And here he was, without a clue what was going on around him.

Placing the pots carefully on the ground, he chased back into the tent. Jacob was busily tending a small fire. He looked up, noticing Jack's angry expression.

'My Lord Burnside? What is it?'

Jack shook his head impatiently. 'There's something weird going on in Asfah – but you know that already.'

'There is, indeed, much sadness in this little town. As yet, I do not know why.' Jacob said.

'You sure about that?'

Jacob stirred the embers into a bright blaze, ignoring Jack's sarcastic tone. 'It may well become clear to me this night. Then, if the Gods are on our side, we will have departed by morning. Please drink some tea, my Lord Burnside,' he said soothingly, 'and you should sleep a few hours. We will eat when the sun sets and, soon after, you will be able to start your journey.'

'What's this?' Jack noticed the carving of a camel lying on a bed of wood shavings.

'I have just finished it. When you find that ingrate, you call Bud, you will leave this in his place.'

'Why?' he said, before realising he already knew the answer. 'I can't leave any trace of my visit?'

'Exactly so, my Lord Burnside, Mendorun must not be alerted to the camel's powers.'

'But this is stupid,' Jack burst out furiously. 'This is the second time you've sent me into a dangerous place, unable to make myself understood. You can't fight sorcery with a boy and a camel. Can't you send in an army?'

'You do not understand.'

'THEN MAKE ME UNDERSTAND,' he shouted, forgetting he could be heard through the thin walls of the tent.

Jacob leapt precipitately to his feet. Swiftly crossing the narrow space, he lifted the tent flap and peered out. He stood there listening. Satisfied, he closed it again returning to his seat by the fire.

'I'm sorry, Jacob, I lost it,' mumbled Jack ashamed, aware his outburst might have serious repercussions if it had been overheard.

Jacob waved his hands in the air dismissing the incident. 'It was no matter.'

'But you only ever tell me half a story. It's a repeat of last time. I find out as I go along.'

Jacob stretched out his hands palms uppermost, expressing his genuine bewilderment.

'But how else should I fight the evil with which Mendorun surrounds himself? With an army, you say? An army of one-thousand men to battle against an army of one thousand and one? That is not the way.'

'Then what is?'

'The dominance of power.'

'How can you expect me to understand something like that?'

'You must work it out, my Lord Burnside, you have all the clues.'

Jack groaned miserably. 'Well … um … you said that Mendorun wants to make himself more and more powerful.' He spoke slowly, wondering what Jacob meant. 'And you can't control him, unless your power is even stronger. *Oh, I get it,*' he exclaimed. 'It's Bud. He's a big part of your power. And if Bud's fallen into Mendorun's hands, you're scuppered. *But there has to be another way*. It's stupid sending someone like me.'

'But, of course. Did you think the fire was only for food? Come – sit here.' Jacob ferreted in his sleeve producing the small box. He opened it and taking out a pinch of white powder threw it into the fire.

Reluctantly Jack sat. His mind was in turmoil, whirling round and round as he tried to develop arguments to resist Jacob's will, sensing it overriding his own.

Jacob walked round the fire speaking softly. The words floated into the air, like the words of a song. Against his will, Jack's arguments fell away. His mind began to absorb the gentle, soothing sounds; the cells and electrical conduits to his brain filling with the guttural syllables of the strange language. Still Jacob spoke, the words dancing in the flames. Gradually the golden syllables began to make sense, Jack reading them as easily as if a pen had written them in the air. The words drifted away tumbling one by one into the fire, flames flicking upwards to devour them.

'I feel weird,' Jack said, his head spinning, like the words being consumed among the ashes.

Jacob shrugged and, bending down, placed a small pan of water on the fire to boil. 'You are speaking in my tongue.'

'*What Arabic! You've got to be joking.*'

Jacob bowed, amusement briefly parting the frowning brows. 'So now you can enter the palace, seek out that accurs-ed camel, understand all their secrets, and tell me of them when you return. And since you have lingering doubts as to my powers …'

A loud crashing of pots cut his words in half. Spears pierced the tent flap ripping it to shreds. Guards thrust aside the tattered remnants, forcing their way in. Their spears pricked against the robes of the two figures seated by the fire, freezing them into immobility.

Chapter Eight

Captured

The noise of shouting hurt Jack's ears, and for a second or two he couldn't understand what was being said – then he did.

'STAY STILL – DON'T MOVE – WHAT ARE YOU DOING HERE?'

Hiding a mouthful of rotten teeth behind his matted beard, the man stuck his face into Jack's. His breath stank of garlic and cheap tobacco, his sword poking and prying even into the cushions on which they were sitting. He tipped the dish of food into the fire and a scalding hiss of steam flew into the air.

'What are you doing here, merchant?' he bellowed.

Laboriously, Jacob levered himself to his feet. Jack watched him change into a querulous, frightened old man; so disabled as to have problems getting up. As he made his painful journey towards standing upright, he lifted one hand into the air, as if offering something to the Gods. It was done so naturally, as if he were simply straightening out his bent old arm or folding back the sleeve of his robe. But Jack had spotted the box resting on the palm of his hand, then the empty hand falling back down to his side. He finally stumbled upright, his bleary, rheumy eyes under an old man's visage fixed on the officer.

Jack rose equally slowly, carefully covering the wooden carving with his foot. Placing a hand on the ground to help him up, he slipped the statue into the folds of his voluminous robe.

'My Lord, I did not mean to offend,' whined Jacob. 'I am but a poor seller of pots, seeking to sell my wares.'

'Shut up, you. Take the boy!'

'But ...' began Jack, his insides dissolving with fear.

'SILENCE!'

The tent became silent except for the intermittent sound of breaking pots. Guards seized Jack's arms, marching him towards the tent opening. For a second, Jacob's eyes locked with his.

'You don't belong here,' screamed the officer.

'Yes, my Lord! No, my Lord! I will remove myself from your sight at once, my Lord. But the boy ... I am but an old man. I need his strong arm to lean on.'

'Lean on your stick, old man, and thank your gods I don't put an end to your miserable existence right now. The boy comes with us.'

A scene of utter desolation met their eyes. Shards of pottery lay in piles on the ground, where the guards had rampaged through the stall smashing everything within sight. Jack, held firmly in a cruel grip, could only watch as they paused in their game to make fun of the old man, herding him at the point of a spear onto the waiting camel.

A horse-drawn cart waited, its sides and roof constructed from horizontal wooden bars, intertwined with others running vertically. A sandaled foot caught Jack violently in the small of his back and, with a cry of fright, he landed face-down on the floor of the cart. Impatiently, the driver flicked the end of his whip at the broken-down nag in the shafts. Jack's captors jeered as the vehicle jerked into motion sending him sprawling again. Silently, he raised himself up on his knees, gazing in despair at the trotting camel already disappearing into the distance.

Jack waited until the sand had swallowed up the moving shape. Bitterly angry with himself; only too aware it was his stupidity that had caused their downfall. Words shouted and not understood in this town, where anything out of the ordinary was to be feared. *Well, look on the bright side*, he told himself bravely, *at least you no longer have to worry about venturing into Mendorun's den on your own. You even have an armed escort.*

He wasn't the only occupant of the moving prison. Three boys shared the space, the two smallest wearing raggedy old shorts and a T-shirt. Both were bare-headed, with thick dark hair in need of cutting. The tallest of the three was dressed like Jack in a tunic. His head was covered with a large piece of cloth falling down over his shoulders, like a badge of office, and secured by a stout piece of string. Bracing themselves against the wooden uprights, they stared unmoving at the ground. And they'd been there a while. The fingertips gripping the wooden bars were white and bloodless, the rough cart lurching and stumbling from one pothole to the next. Jack grimaced and tucked his robe under him, the wooden floor blisteringly-hot under the afternoon sun.

The two smaller boys had not stirred, even when Jack had nearly fallen on them. He saw their lips moving silently and continuously, and guessed they were praying. He started to say something when the boy opposite placed a warning finger against his lips. His eyes flashed momentarily towards the guards walking behind the cage, their spears bright in the sunlight.

For what seemed like hours, they bumped along the unmade track. No one bothered to give the prisoners water, although the guards drank steadily from leather gourds hung from the back of the cart, passing the life-giving substance between them. By the time they came within hailing distance of the dark fortress walls, Jack felt bruised and battered as if he were a punch bag. He might well have been for all the notice the driver took, as careless for the safety of the occupants of his cart as he was of the animal in the shafts.

With a loud grating noise, the menacing spikes of a portcullis were drawn up to let the cart pass through. A moment later they hurtled viciously down into the ground, cutting off their view of the open desert, with Asfah only a speck in the distance. As scared as he had ever been in his life, Jack glanced at the two small boys, their lips moving in an unending succession of prayers, and hoped his face wasn't as white as theirs.

The cart halted. With a loud rattle, the padlock and chain were lifted off and the barred gate opened. A spear entered, prodding the four boys as if they were cattle.

Huddled together for protection, they climbed awkwardly down onto the paved floor of the courtyard. Spears butted against their shoulders, leaving them with no option but to follow the driver, making his way between a line of stone columns. The man ducked into a doorway on the far side.

The sound of voices drifted through the open door. Jack stopped dead. Panic-stricken, he recognised the silken tones.

'I do not like excuses. Four you say, *only four*? You promised me *six*.'

It can't be! Waves of horror swept over Jack and a taste of bile surged into his mouth. He would be recognised. Digging his toes into the stone path, he tried to resist being pushed forward. The three boys cannoned into him desperate to escape the sharp tips of the spears.

'B … B … But your Excellency. These are strong boys. *Very* strong,' babbled the driver.

The ground swirled becoming blurred, Jack's brain blasted into pieces as if someone had let off a squib inside his head.

SALADIN!

As if it were yesterday, Jack recalled the tyrant's last words to him. "*And you will not live to see the light of day. That thought, Mr Burnside, gives me great pleasure.*" Now, they were about to come true.

The driver reappeared in the doorway, obsequious and gushing, his arm ushering someone out into the yard. Saladin. Only of medium height, rolls of fat bulged through the silk of his robe, his face sallow and unhealthy, with deep shadows under his eyes. Black and soulless, they flicked round the offering like a snake about to devour its prey.

'*Me Lord, 'ave mercy, it's not me you want. I don't belong wiv the overs.*'

The boy, whose gesture had prevented Jack speaking, barged into him shoving him to one side. He flung himself on the ground, plucking wildly at the hem of Saladin's robe.

'*Me Lord, please 'ave pity. Send me 'ome. Me mover needs me to work for me brovers and sisters. They will starve – me Lord – take these free – they'll serve ye but let me go, I beg you. I don't belong 'ere and I want me mover.*'

The boy's voice rose louder and louder as he begged and whined, crying aloud, almost ripping Saladin's robe with his frantic clawing.

'They will do,' Saladin hissed. Contemptuously, he kicked the snivelling figure aside. 'Take them below. Bring me six tomorrow and do not fail.' With one final kick of disgust, at the boy blubbing at his feet, he headed back into the room and shut the door.

'Get up!' yelled the driver, using his spear to prise the boy off the ground.

The boy rose silently to his feet, so calm Jack couldn't believe he'd been a grovelling heap only a second before. *How? Why?* Almost at once he knew the answer as the boy drew close to his side, shielding him from the gaze of anyone looking out of the window. For some reason, the boy had purposely stepped in to save him.

Jack touched the boy on his forearm. 'Thanks,' he breathed and was rewarded with a half-smile of acknowledgement.

But Saladin here! He had to get out and fast. The sky had become a mass of pinks and reds as the sun slipped towards the horizon. Once it was dark, surely Jacob would send Betsy.

The guards, using their spears freely, herded the four boys down some steps on the far side of the courtyard. At the bottom of the steep flight, Jack peered over his shoulder for one final glimpse of the sky, its brightness lost in the darkness of the tunnel opening up before them.

Focussing his attention on their surroundings, Jack headed into the tunnel, as slowly as the bellowed curses would allow. Sensing a reason behind his odd behaviour the boy, who had saved him, dragged his steps in time with Jack's, leaving the youngsters to bear the brunt of the spear pricks. Terrified, they constantly barged into the laggards in front.

A blow struck Jack in the back and he turned protesting, 'Watch it,' before registering there was space between him and the boy walking behind. *Then who? Bud? Could it be?* Jack's heart leapt with total, uncontrollable joy but not one single spec showed on his face. His expression of pained innocence was one he had perfected in his bedroom mirror at home, and now could call up at will.

A tunnel opened up on his left; water dripping from the black basalt walls leaving puddles on the uneven ground. Somewhere down that tunnel was his friend.

'*Get a move on.*' The spear tip reached its target and he hurried on, stumbling slightly in an attempt to dodge the sharp tip slicing into his shoulders.

Bent almost double, the boys were herded under a low stone arch into a cave lit by oil lamps. Reflecting off the chiselled face of the walls, they gave a smoky, flickering light. The cave wasn't a natural phenomenon, like the ones Jack had visited on holiday, with stalagmites and stalactites; this had been hewn out of the mountain. It was empty, except for a pile of rags in one corner and a large cage, identical to the one they had just left.

The guards circled round them, leaving the boys in no doubt they had reached their destination. Pushing water and dishes of rice in after them, they shoved the four boys into their new prison. Then padlocking the cage, they left; their footsteps fading as they headed towards the steps leading up into the fresh air.

Chapter Nine

The Cage

For a moment no one spoke in case it was a trick, but the silence persisted. Eventually Jack stirred, stretching his arms and legs cramped with the tension of holding himself upright. Bending down, he poured some water from the pitcher drinking thirstily.

'Here,' Jack whispered to the two boys their lips still moving in prayer. He held out a cup. 'Have a drink. You're safe now. Eat the rice too.' One of the boys looked up, his eyes beseeching. 'Yes, we'll get out of here,' he replied with as much assurance as he could muster. 'But it could be a while, and you need to eat and drink and sleep, in that order. Will you do that?'

The boy passed the little dish of food to his friend; their eyes constantly on the move, never still for a moment, shifting nervously round the cavern as they nibbled at the soft grains.

'You used to kids?' said the youth who had helped him. He drank some water then sat himself beside Jack to eat his rice.

'Yes, I am – well was,' Jack corrected himself hastily. 'They're really scared – worse than us. By the way, thanks.'

'I 'ad to do somefin, mate, thought you was goin' to pee yerself when ye saw that bloke. Oo is 'e anyway?'

'Saladin? He's the uncle of a friend of mine. Some uncle! He dumped my friend and his father in prison and left them there to rot. Not nice. If he recognises me, he'll have me roasted over a slow fire, *and I'm not joking*,' Jack added, unable to conceal a shudder at the thought.

'Didn't think ye was, still we'll 'ave to think somefin' up. I can't try that again. Me name's Khan, by the way.' The boy didn't bother to look up, concentrating on eating his food.

'So how did they capture you?' Jack gazed at him, wondering how anyone could remain so calm and composed locked in a cage. Slightly older than Jack, his skin was dark and swarthy as if he worked outside; his hair under his head-wrap jet black and curly. 'What about your family?'

The boy shook his head. His mouth was full of rice and he chewed the grains carefully before replying.

'Ain't got none. Must 'ave once but I'm what's called a street urchin. That lot …' he jerked his thumb towards the tunnel, 'was trawlin' the street. I lucked out. And you?'

'I was at the town, with my … um … grandfather. We sell pots.'

'Wha'ch ye called?'

'Jack Burnside,' Jack answered without thinking.

'Jack Burnside! That's an English name. It's the name of that poncy footballer. Why 'ave ye got an English name?' Khan accused. He glared at Jack suspiciously. On the streets, survival depended on mistrust of anything out of the norm and Jack's answer didn't fit.

'It's a long story,' Jack said. 'My real name's Abdullah. My friends call me Jack, 'cos I play football like him.' He grinned innocently aware that the less anyone knew about him, the safer he'd be. 'Look, we've got to get out of this place.'

'Ye're not jokin'. Shouldn't be a problem once that lot's asleep.' Khan nodded in the general direction of the steps. 'But we 'ave to take them prayer-mutterers, they wouldn't last five minutes wivout us.'

'OK, but I've got to find someone first,' Jack agreed somewhat distractedly, wondering how they were going to escape from the cage. He rattled the bars hoping to discover a loose one, but they all fitted tightly.

The moment the words were out, he knew he'd blown it. Khan's face changed, becoming openly hostile.

''Ere, wait a minute. I thought you was captured. It don't add up.'

'Oh hell! I know it doesn't, but it's a long story.'

'Ye said that before. So *what is this story and why, 'ave ye got an English name?'* Khan peered at Jack. He flinched back keeping his face in shadow. 'And what's more ye're the funniest lookin' Arab I've ever seen.'

'There's lots of fair Arabs,' Jack protested.

'Not round 'ere, there ain't. So where d'ye come from and don't give me that, *it's a long story* crap, 'cos if it comes to a scrap I know 'oo I'm backin'.'

That's where you're wrong, mate, Jack murmured under his breath. 'I've got doubts about you, too,' he countered. 'For starters, why are you so flippin' calm? That doesn't make sense. We could all be dead in the morning and you're eating your dinner as if you were at home.'

Nervously, the two little boys buried their faces deep in their chests, displaying – as dogs do – that they weren't part of the fight.

'OK, I'll make a deal wiv ye. Tell me 'oo ye're lookin' for and I'll tell ye why I'm eatin' me dinner calmly like. Deal?'

'OK!'

'But you go first.'

Jack took a deep breath. 'It *is* a long story. *Hey!'* He raised his hands defensively. *'But I'll tell you some of it,'* he quickly added, noticing the sneer on Khan's face. 'My real name *is* Jack Burnside but I speak the Arabic language. Anyway, this place is total evil. Its ruler is a Sheikh Mendorun and if he's going round the countryside capturing kids, there's no prizes for guessing he must be the most screwed-up evil man you will ever meet – bar Saladin. The thing is – some friends and I had a run in with Saladin a few months back. He'd overthrown the real ruler of Sudana.'

'Sudana? Never 'eard of it.'

'It's a small kingdom the other side of these mountains,' Jack said. 'It was only by luck we got it back. Now my friends think that Mendorun is planning something really mind-blowing. They've come here to discover what – and I've come with them. A friend of mine is trapped somewhere in this fortress. We were trying to work out how to rescue him, when I was captured.'

'Look, Khan,' Jack hesitated, hoping his story would be believed. Even to him it sounded far-fetched. 'I know you don't altogether trust me, but I promise you we're on the same side.'

Khan's coal-black eyes bored into Jack's light hazel ones.

'OK! Like ye said – I don't trust ye, but I'll work wiv ye and I'll be honest wiv ye, and I expect ye to be the same. But I'll still be watchin' ye closely – good enuff.'

'Good enough. Now you go.'

'I can open the cage door,' Khan said, calmly eating.

'*You can do what?*' Jack gaped at him. 'But how?'

'No idea.' Khan licked the grains from his empty dish. 'But I can. So we wait till that lot's asleep, then we simply walk out'a 'ere.'

'It's not going to be as easy as you think,' Jack said, remembering the portcullis, with its panels of burnished metal rattling into place. 'But we'll find a way.'

''Oo you got to rescue?'

Jack screwed up his face, well aware that what he was going to say sounded bonkers. 'It's not actually a person. It's more of a thing.'

'Blimey, it must be gold.'

'Not gold, no – but it's very precious. Anyway, if you can open the door for me, will you wait here while I search for it?'

The boy shook his head. 'If yew're goin' wanderin' round this place, I'm comin' wiv ye, in case ye decide to leave wivout tellin' me. Anyway, ye need me.'

'I don't see why,' Jack said irritably. 'You'd be more use keeping an eye on them.'

Khan glanced at the two boys crouched in the corner. 'Them prayer-mutterers! They'll 'ave to come wiv us. We can't leave 'em 'ere, they'll die of fright.'

'Jeez! *Haven't you got it yet!* We're in a fortress manned by dozens of armed men. Just 'cos you can open locks, it doesn't mean we can go wandering round this place, as if we're on a picnic. One of us might get away with it; I doubt two will *and I am damned sure four can't,*' Jack thundered angrily. 'We'd be spotted before we'd gone a dozen metres and I *absolutely have* to find this thing first.'

'Why?'

Jack, faced with the question, nearly flipped. 'Because it's something I owe my life too,' he admitted reluctantly.

'OK! That's good enuff for me.'

'It is?' said Jack, unbelieving.

'I might be a street kid wivout any learnin' but I understand about 'onour. Our gangs work on 'onour. Still I'm comin' wiv ye – deal?'

'OK, but *you* have to tell the boys something. *Prayer-mutterers,* did you call them?' Khan nodded. 'Cool name by the way.'

Khan grinned, a crooked sort of smile – lop-sided – as if only half of his face wanted to be friendly.

'I tell you what,' Jack said. 'We could use those rags and make a couple of bodies out of them. Then, if a guard does come along he'll think we're sleeping.'

Khan stretched his hands towards the lock. With a loud click the padlock sprang open, the gate swinging silently on its hinges. Astonished, Jack slithered to the ground. He listened to Khan's calm voice explaining to the two boys that they weren't in league with the devil, and they really would help them reach safety. Bending low, he slid under the barrier of rock, risking a quick peek into the corridor. It remained silent and empty.

Darting into the shadows, he sorted through the pile of rags, hoping to salvage some pieces big enough to pack into rolls.

'Jack,' Khan's stage whisper reached him across the cave. 'Where 'ave ye gone? I thought …'

Jack stepped out of the shadow, a bundle of rags in his hands. 'See if you can make something that resembles a person sleeping, with this little lot.' He darted back across the floor to collect another armful. 'Are those two OK with this?' He jerked his head towards the two boys, their faces full of fear.

'Jack?'

'*Shush!* What is it?'

'Ye've disappeared.'

'I haven't. I'm right here.' he snapped irritably. He stepped into the lamplight, glaring across the room at Khan. '*What's the matter with you?* I said we'd go together, I'm not about to run off and leave you.'

The black eyes met his across the pile of rags. 'So ye said but I'm 'avin' trouble believin' ye.'

'Believing me, why?' Jack pulled some pieces of sacking from the pile, tossing them over to Khan.

''Cos now I've opened the door, ye disappear.'

'I do what?'

'Disappear,' Khan repeated loudly.

Jack stopped in the middle of the floor. 'Can you see me now?'

'But …'

'But nothing,' he retorted. 'I'm not going to vanish. OK?'

'When you go into the shadow ye do,' Khan said calmly.

Stunned, Jack could only gape. 'You mean, I …'

'Disappear. Yes.'

'How?'

'Ye sort'a fade.'

'You mean you can't see me *at all*?' Jack said, feeling light-headed.

'Come on, Jack, stop playin' games – it's not somefin' ye wouldn't notice.'

Jack shook his head miserably. 'I promise you, Khan, this is as much a surprise to me as it is to you. This morning I was quite normal and … *Jacob!*' he yelped, remembering the sorcerer in the middle of telling him something, when the guards burst in. 'Thank God!'

Khan continued to prod and punch the rags into the shape of a body, studying Jack closely all the time. Jack, clutching a bundle of rags, kicked the rest into a heap hurrying back to the cage.

'Look, you two – what's your name by the way?'

'Abu, sir,' the littlest boy said. 'My friend is called Shahi.'

'OK! I understand you're frightened,' Jack gabbled excitedly, 'but I promise you we're going to escape. All you've got to do is pretend to be sleeping.'

'*I told 'em that already*,' said Khan, his manner belligerent.

Jack spun round to face him, angered by his tone. 'Well, I've got something to add, *OK*?'

'OK! But I'm watchin' ye.'

Jack ignored him. 'Can you do that?'

Shahi instantly lay down.

Jack yanked him back onto his feet. 'Not yet, when I say. Khan, give me your hand quick.' He tugged the reluctant boy with him into the shadows. 'Can you see us?' he called.

There was silence. Impatiently, Jack stepped back into the light. Abu and Shahi stared at him, their eyes as wide as saucers. They shook their heads, already beginning a prayer asking God for deliverance from evil.

'Khan, if you can open the doors I can get us out,' Jack said, as excited as if he'd climbed the highest mountain in the world or scored the winning goal in the World Cup. 'Only one problem, it's got to be dark.'

'OK, I'm not movin' till ye tell me how ye can disappear all of a sudden?'

'Do you know how you can open doors?'

'No, but what's that got to do with anyfin'.'

'Because I hadn't a clue I could do this until a minute ago. I told you I had some powerful friends. One of them's a sorcerer.' Khan's expression changed to one of disbelief. 'You can believe that or not, but I'll prove it to you. Anyhow, this is his work.'

'Ye said Jacob?'

'Yeah, that's his name, and he's trying to stop Mendorun before he becomes unstoppable.'

'And this Mendorun bloke?'

'Trust me, you don't want to go there. Come on. We'd better hurry. We daren't leave these two for long, in case the guards come back.'

Chapter Ten

The Room of Lights

The two boys crept silently down the tunnel, the atmosphere spooky in the half-light.

'Ye sure about this?' Khan whispered.

'You saw the prayer-mutterers' faces. They couldn't have been more scared if they'd seen the devil himself or, in our case, *not seen him*. But I'm not sure about the four of us. I've only got two hands!'

'Yeah, could be a problem.'

'But the odds will be much higher if I find my friend,' Jack added, feeling optimistic. He peered down the straight rockshaft, the light from the oil lamps reflecting in the pools of water like bright nuggets of gold. 'I think it's this one.'

'Can we be 'eard?' breathed Khan.

'Couldn't say, but I'm not chancing it. This bit's *got* to go right. They can't notice we've been here.'

Grasping Khan's hand, the two boys slipped into the shadowy tunnel, its roof so low they could sense its weight pressing down on their heads. A moment later, a stout wooden door blocked their way, an iron padlock holding it firmly closed.

Immediately, Khan's hands stretched towards the lock and it clicked open. The noise reverberated up and down the empty tunnel, freezing the two boys in their tracks. Cautiously, Jack eased open the door and peered in.

The room was vast, its edges lost among shadows, its centre a sparkling golden carousel with shafts of brilliant light pouring down from the cave roof, fusing the floor to the ceiling. Dotted about the space were tall black stands; reminding Jack of the lectern their headmaster used in assembly. Some were simply that – empty stands; those within the carousel basking in light, like sunbathers on a beach. Others had things standing on them. Jack gazed in disbelief at the monstrous shape, its talons twice the length of his fingers.

Against his will, his eyes crawled upwards examining the yellow scaly legs; fine black down dissolving into the rich, fluorescent black of the chest and wing feathers. Above them, a black beak jutted menacingly. Suddenly, a gleam of brightness struck him from the partially-closed lids. He jerked back out of range, behind the wooden door, cannoning into Khan who'd been craning over his shoulder.

'What the …' Khan noticed Jack's face, almost green under its tan. 'You OK?'

Jack leant over, his hands clasping his middle, taking some deep breaths – completely forgetting his action rendered Khan visible again.

'What scared ye, go on, tell me,' Khan's piercing whisper brought Jack out of his daze.

'Birds. I saw three of them.'

'*Birds! Birds!* What d'ye mean birds?'

Impatiently, Khan pushed past him and stuck his head round the door. He flinched back. '*Blimey*! They aren't 'alf big. That one's got an 'ead the size of a football. What are they?'

'Crows, I think. I've seen them before – but nothing like this.'

'Can they see us?'

Jack shook his head miserably. 'I think they're sleeping.'

'Then we go in silent-like, grab ye're friend and get the 'ell out'a there.'

'I agree,' said Jack, a wan smile flickering across his face, wishing he could borrow some of Khan's coolness.

Like ghosts, the two boys slipped into the room. They edged cautiously around the shadowy perimeter, alert for any sign that the bird had spotted them; its head slumped forwards over its barrel chest dozing. A gleam of light from the half-closed lids halted them in their tracks. They drew closer to the wall and waited before moving on again.

Jack had spotted three of the giant birds when he opened the door. Ten more came into view, among a dozen or so empty shafts of light. There was no longer any doubt about the extent of Mendorun's ambitions or – if he could fill the empty shafts – his power.

In the centre of the carousel stood the small, almost insignificant, silhouette of a camel, its head held proudly, defiantly, against the black menace surrounding it.

Overjoyed, Jack pulled out the wooden carving he'd kept so carefully hidden.

'Ye've gotta be kiddin, right!' Khan gazed at it in disbelief. 'We came all this way for a poxy wooden camel. I've sold wood carvin's betta'en that to earn me dinner,' he added scornfully.

Jack's eyes flashed and his hand curled into a fist before he could stop it. *What did a street boy know about anything?*

'Look, I'm going out there,' he said, almost spitting the words out, he was so angry. 'You can stay here, for all I care. The birds are sleeping so you're quite safe. Besides, I need both my hands for this. Don't forget *you can't see me either*, so don't be surprised when that *poxy statue*, as you call it, levitates.'

Without bothering to wait for a reply, Jack loosed his hand, cautiously edging past the sleeping birds. A sudden gleam from an eye unnerved him, his hands shaking so badly he nearly dropped the wooden carving. He was halfway across the room before he noticed a change in the light. A section of the roof was missing, replaced by stars.

Up close, the light from the carousel was blinding. Jack flinched back, shielding his eyes with his arm. Keeping them half-closed, he slowly stretched out his hand, testing the light beam with the tips of his fingers. He half expected it to burn like the sun and was surprised to feel only a gentle warmth. There came a sudden rustle of feathers and Jack froze. Abruptly, he remembered that he would be visible, and a target for anyone in the room, while he swapped the carvings. Withdrawing his hand, he checked again, noticing Khan in the shadows and the sleeping birds but no one else. Nervously, he stepped into the light edging round the empty stands. Lifting up the warm sandalwood body of the camel, he placed the replica in exactly the same spot. He'd done it.

He ran back across the floor and grabbed Khan's hand. 'Let's get the hell out of here.'

Chapter Eleven

The Lair of the Sorcerer

The words SAFETY and ESCAPE flashed like neon signs from the rock walls, as Jack and Khan tore up the tunnel. Alarmed, the two youngsters sat bolt upright, relief sweeping over their faces as they recognised their companions, who – scary or not – seemed their best chance of getting back to their homes.

Jack, leaving Khan to unlock the cage, placed Bud on the floor under the soft lamplight.

'Come on, Bud, do your party trick,' he whispered, waiting in eager anticipation for the sneering face to pop out of the wall. 'Come on, Bud, don't let me down,' he begged, changing the camel's position first to more light, then to more shadow. 'Bud, I need you,' he pleaded.

He picked up the carving, talking to it as if it had been alive. He tried again, the small shadow clear and bright in the lamplight. Nothing happened. It didn't move. It didn't grow till it overlapped the wall and allow a pair of mournful eyes to come to life.

A feeling of desperation overtook Jack. He felt empty inside, as if his guts had melted. Why didn't Bud respond? It had to be something bad, because Bud had never failed him before. Snatching a long piece of stout cloth from the pile, he rolled the statue carefully in it. He must reach Jacob without delay. He would know what to do.

'What the 'ell are ye doin'?' Khan's voice broke into Jack's thoughts.

'It didn't work. We'll have to make it on our own.'

'What d'ye mean, what didn't work?'

'The camel – it comes to life.'

'Pull the other one. Ye've wasted hours poncin' around 'ere for a stupid wooden camel, and now ye pretend it comes to life,' Khan scoffed. 'I could 'ave bin out of 'ere and them two,' he pointed at the boys, '*and* 'alf way home if I 'adn't listened to you and yer stupid, *stupid* friend that you 'ad to rescue. And guess what – *it's not even valuable.*'

'If it had worked you'd be sneering on the other side of your face,' Jack retorted, busily tying a knot in the fabric to prevent the wooden camel falling out. 'If we hurry, we can still do it. Come on, Khan, you said you'd trust me.'

'*Trust you! I'd rather trust a tarantula.*'

Jack's fist caught Khan smack on the side of his jaw.

Next second, the two boys were rolling round the floor – fists flying – aware, deep in the recesses of their mind, that this fight had to be conducted in total silence. Not a sound broke the tension in the air, except for soft panting, and a gasp from Jack as Khan head-butted him.

Jack sprang upright fast, kicking upwards into Khan's chest. Winded, Khan lost his balance tumbling backwards onto a pile of rags, gasping for breath. Jack, using the momentum of his kick, catapulted his body down on to him. But Khan hadn't lived in the street without learning how to fight. As Jack launched himself, he twisted away. Slippery as an eel, he was back on his feet and, despite his lack of breath, immediately dived on top of Jack's falling body, raining blows to the side of his head.

The two small boys gazed at them in disbelief, their hands clamped over their ears, their frightened eyes repeatedly swivelling towards the archway, convinced guards with spears would appear any second. Jack, flinging Khan off his back, regained his feet and turned panting, his fists ready to strike again.

'You 'ad enough,' Khan rubbed his ribs where Jack had kicked him.

'No! You?' Jack spotted the cut lip of his opponent and a smile twisted his mouth.

'Please, sirs!'

A hand grasped Jack's sleeve another tugging at Khan, both combatants so hyped-up neither wanted to break eye contact. It was Khan that looked away first.

'Let's get out'a 'ere.'

'Khan, *I'm sorry*,' said Jack, instantly remorseful. He rubbed his cheek, suddenly aware the side of his face stung from contact with Khan's fist. 'But *never* say anything about the camel. He's off limits. Look, we've got to work together but, once we're out, you can go your way and I'll go mine. We need never meet again.'

'Suits me fine.'

'Yeah, me too. But until then we've got to get along. Shake?' Jack held out his hand. Khan, hesitated for a second, then took it.

'But I'm still watchin' ye, so don't go thinkin' anyfing's changed.'

Jack picked up the bundle containing the camel. 'Whatever you think of me, Khan, if for some reason I don't make it, this parcel has to. Will you at least promise me that?'

Khan nodded. 'So 'ow do we get out?'

'You go first – I'll hang onto your shoulder. The boys will have to walk behind. Listen you two,' Jack said. 'You saw me disappear. So hold on tight to me and no one will see you, *but they can hear you*. Not a word, understand?' The two boys immediately grabbed Jack's shoulder, Shahi's face a picture of misery.

Hugging the wall tightly, they ducked under the archway, Khan checking first to make sure the tunnel was empty. Jack gripped his shoulder, feeling Abu and Shahi breathing down his neck. His anger rumbled on. It hadn't subsided much and he still felt it, although mostly at himself, aware he wouldn't have fought if it had involved anything but Bud. He couldn't believe the camel hadn't come alive, wondering if its catatonic state was somehow connected to the room of lights. And what if he had been completely destroyed? With all that to worry about, Khan's sneering had been the last straw. *Still, how stupid could you get!* Well, as soon as they were free, Khan could take his stupid face elsewhere and good riddance.

Their pace was slow. Like a discombobulated crab, they crawled along the tunnel, visible as they passed under the oil lamps where the light was strongest, disappearing as they moved into the shadow. It was painful-going with Abu and Shahi constantly butting into Jack, their fingers digging sharply into his shoulders. He stumbled as, yet again, one of them trod on his heels. Finally, they reached the flight of steps into the courtyard.

'I'd better go first, to check it's safe,' he whispered.

'Not wivout me ye're not.' Khan glared mutinously, his black eyes boring into him.

'I have to do this alone,' Jack pleaded, noticing Khan's belligerent expression. 'What happens if there's light and people up there? We daren't risk it.' He untied the bundle at his waist. 'Here, a pledge of good faith. If you've got my camel, from now on I'll be keeping my eye on you.'

Taking the parcel, Khan ducked into the dark well behind the steps, pushing the two boys in first, understanding that Jack wasn't about to leave the carving behind, not when he'd gone to so much trouble to retrieve it.

Cautiously, Jack slipped up the flight of steps and out into the courtyard, away from the safety of the tunnel entrance. Overhead the moon sailed majestically through the sky, exploring the silent rock face with its silver light. Automatically, he looked for his watch, before remembering he'd left it with his clothes in the cave.

The courtyard was empty and bare, and so vast it could have housed an entire army. Dark satanic stone, torn from the mountainside, had been used to build the towering fortress walls, their symmetry broken only by twin guard towers. Flanking the main gate, these held the iron ribs of the portcullis in their bowels. On either side, cupboard-like rooms burrowed deep into the solid walls, gloomy and cavernous. A place for dark deeds. Sinister and brooding, even the moonlight failed to make it beautiful.

Jack flitted silently along the walls seeking a small gate. There had to be one, it was simply a question of where. There was no way guards would raise and lower the portcullis, every time one or two people needed to enter or leave the fortress.

Behind him, rubbing shoulders with the mountainside appeared the dark shape of a temple. Only the facade stood clear of the rocks, as if the mountain had tried to swallow it whole. Rows of pillars, as rigid as sentries on duty, obscured the entire ground floor. At each corner, they thrust their way to the top of the building, to be crowned by a square capital decorated with palm leaves, which supported the triangular pediment.

A light shone from a window on the first floor, a pool of silver reflected onto the courtyard floor. Jack studied its unblinking brightness, wishing he were brave enough to go up there and find out who was still awake. He turned away, angry with himself for wasting time; Khan would be up for another fight if he didn't hurry back.

At ground level, the columns provided shade in the heat of the day. Now, they provided shadow and safety for Jack. He ran the entire length of the building, his light sandals making little sound on the stone ground. He headed for a wide buttress of rock, which adjoined and partially concealed the ramparts beyond, almost shouting aloud his joy at discovering the little wooden gate tucked behind it.

Silently retracing his steps, Jack slipped past the dozen or so windows on the ground floor. They were open to the air, none of them having glass, since burglars were the last thing on anyone's mind in an armed camp. He paused hovering, his weight already transferred onto his toes for the next step. The tantalising square of light beckoned. Without knowing how or why, he found himself sliding through the window nearest to him.

Inside, dozens of men lay asleep on the floor. Cautiously, Jack tiptoed through them and out into a corridor. Built of the same black stone as the outer walls, feeble rays of moonlight trickled through the windows making it possible to find his way through the darkness. Abruptly, the passage widened out into a large rectangular hallway, the carpeted treads of a magnificent staircase floating upwards. On the far side the corridor, like a black pathway, faded into the distance.

Deciding that only the kitchens and armoury were likely to be housed on the ground floor, and it was not worth investigating, Jack sprinted up the stairs. The wide landing was festooned with crystal chandeliers and gilt mirrors. Reaching the top, he moved cautiously, conscious that each step was taking him closer to danger and he would remain invisible so long as kept in the shadow. If he dared approach too close to any light, like a moth burned by a flame he would instantly be seen. Yet something urged him on, a force outside himself thrusting his feet forwards.

Six doors opened out of the landing but which concealed the lighted room? The carpet pile was too dense for stray beams to trickle through and provide a clue. Jack shut his eyes, struggling to visualise the front of the building. Nervously, he touched the handle of the second door along. *What if he was wrong?* He eased the handle down, releasing it as the door moved slowly inwards. Only darkness showed. Relieved, he pressed the door open with his fingertips, following it in.

He was in a huge salon, with fancy drapes at each of the half-dozen windows. The room appeared ghostly in the moonlight, its rows of couches standing empty. A faint sliver of light trickled across the carpet; the door in the far wall slightly ajar. He heard the sound of a cup being replaced on its saucer, and smelt tobacco. There were people in that room, although it was impossible to tell how many; and he daren't ease the door open any further, it was far too risky. He was about to retrace his steps, when a voice stopped him.

'And the small matter of my brother Sal-ah?'

There came a rustle of silken garments as if someone had got to their feet, then the soft foot fall that slippers make on a carpet.

'You are meaning the poison, Prince Saladin? That will soon be arranged. Tomorrow night to be exact. At sunset on that day the birds will drop the poison into the palace well.'

'Into the well! But all will die, my esteem-ed Lord. Surely ...'

'*Surely*, Saladin? Surely it matters not if they all die so long as the prince and his whelp die. You would have had to kill them in any event, for you could never gain their loyalty.'

Jack gasped aloud, clamping his hand over his mouth to stifle the noise. He put his ear to the crack, craning to catch the reply. It didn't come, but it didn't matter – he knew what it said.

'And the sorcerer? Does he have power enough to prevent this? I ask humbly, my Lord Mendorun.'

'*Power?* There is no sorcerer living with my power. There were, many moons ago, but I destroyed them all. Nothing can prevent my triumph. Why else have I waited so long? The birds have given me supreme power and now I have destroyed the sorcerer's familiar, he is like a rudderless ship in a storm. And it is *I, Mendorun*, who is the storm.'

Jack didn't wait to hear any more. Bud destroyed, the prince to be poisoned, and everyone to die? *It couldn't be true, it couldn't!*

The phrases beat time in his head, the word *die* marching in tune to his racing feet, as he fled down the elaborately carved staircase and through the sleeping men. He hurled himself through the window into the friendly night air. Hardly caring if he made a noise, he ran for the stairwell, cannoning into Khan.

'About time too,' Khan rubbed his shoulder where he'd scraped it against the wall. 'Thought ye'd scarpered.' He beckoned the two youngsters, who came slowly up the steps not able to see Jack. He immediately took their hands, receiving a relieved smile in return.

'I hadn't but we're going and right now. Something terrible's happened. Come on, let's get out of here.'

Trying not to let his eyes be drawn towards the light, Jack concentrated on his feet; left – right – left – right, the only way he knew to stop Mendorun's evil power invading his head.

'What took ye so long?' Khan's voice broke into the rhythm of his steps.

Jack shook his head. 'There's no time to tell you now, but please, Khan, trust me even if you don't want to.'

'I'm not arguin.' Khan whispered over his shoulder. 'You didn't see yer face when I bumped into ye – scared silly ye was. But what about them?'

Jack took a deep breath. 'Thanks, Khan.' He spoke over his shoulder. 'You know we're in great danger 'cos you were listening. We're going to need every prayer you can think of and keep them coming.'

'But …' began Abu.

'But silently. Like I told you, no noise.'

Chapter Twelve

Escape

A shout of alarm severed the still air, freezing the four boys into statues; the buttress of rock concealing the postern, once again out of reach across the bright, moonlit courtyard.

Jack wished desperately he had Bud with them. He could have passed unseen through the wall, not even bothering with the postern. *If only*. But he wasn't. It was up to him, Jack Burnside of Birmingham, England, to get the four of them to safety. He'd been in tight spots before, *although never this tight*, and always got out of them.

He backed the little group into deep shadow under the wall, aware of how scared the youngsters were, feeling their hands quiver on his shoulders. He gave them a reassuring smile and patted their outstretched arms. Thank heaven, Khan hadn't lost his bottle and was as calm as ever.

Armed men erupted into the courtyard rushing madly about, although not yet in any particular direction. Guards, their spears and swords at the ready, hurried towards the underground maze of tunnels. Others homed in on the ramparts checking the box-like cells beneath. As they finished, they surged across the courtyard towards the building behind them. There was no attempt at silence, their clumsy feet tramping from room to room. Door after door slammed as rooms were entered and searched. Their burning torches pursued a relentless path along the ground floor, the guards ferreting into every corner and every crevice.

A light flared in the room behind. Jack pushed the two young boys to the ground, he and Khan crouching over them. There came the sound of furniture being thrown around, cupboard doors opened and slammed shut. A loud crash made them jump, as something heavy fell to the ground, and one of youngsters began to cry silently. The door banged shut, the bolt grating loudly. Gradually the noise and light faded, moving away to other rooms in the building, leaving those immediately behind in darkness.

For a moment the courtyard was empty.

'Quick, through the window,' Jack whispered.

Khan hoisted Shahi up. It was scary. If anyone had been watching, they would have instantly been spotted and capture would follow within seconds. Abu went next; Khan diving headfirst through the gap as the sound of running feet burst from the underground caves. Jack hurled himself through the open space, Khan reaching up to drag him down to the floor.

They were in a storeroom, one with a door. Jack tried the handle. It was locked.

'We should be safe here. But don't touch anything in case you make a noise.'

''Ow the 'ell do we get out now?' Khan whispered. 'We'd just got out and you got'us back in again.'

'*Don't you think I know that,*' Jack said. 'But they haven't checked the columns yet. Some bright spark is bound to think of them – it's the perfect hiding place.'

'But 'ow the 'ell do we get out now?' Khan repeated.

Close at hand came the sound of running feet on steps. Jack guessed they were combing the ramparts again. Faced with Mendorun, the guards would check each part of the fortress at least twice, with every patch of shadow investigated at spear point.

They heard movement directly outside the window and someone

spoke. 'No, Your Excellency, we believe them to be still underground.'

There came a reply, the words too soft to hear what was said.

'Yes, Your Excellency, if the four boys have run into the tunnels, they cannot escape.'

Little by little, Jack eased himself upright until his nose was level with the window. He caught a glimpse of a guard, but not who he was talking to. Then a tall man came into view, his garments rustling as he walked. His hair, unlike Saladin's oily blackness, was streaked with white, his dark eyes restless and brooding. Jack flinched back into the safety of the wall – Mendorun.

The moon sailed out from behind a small cloud, its white light beaming down and exposing a cicatrix on the sorcerer's face – its twin scars vividly slashed across one cheek. With a great roar of noise he raised his arms, his fingers outstretched, describing a half-circle around him in the air.

'*AWAY!*'

No one stayed to argue. The guards instantly vanished, their running footsteps emphasising the speed of their retreat into the underground caves.

Mendorun drew his arms and hands together, his finger tips curved and touching, as if he held something precious within the circle of his hands. It seemed as if he was about to offer it to the sky. Instead, the opposite happened. His hands opened and his fingers clawed their way upwards to grab the moonbeams and pull them down, smothering them with his hands until the sky was dark.

Jack's knees shook with fright, aware of the awesome power the man wielded, yet unable to drag himself away from the window.

A wind rose up. Gusting strongly, it swept sand from the desert floor, hurling great handfuls of coarse brown particles into the air, leaving sand-filled clouds floating through the night sky.

'Bonticas Sebola'.

As Mendorun's words filled the air, one of the smaller segments ceased its aimless wandering and changed shape. A dark-coloured nucleus, like the head of a tadpole, appeared. Sprouting a tail, it wriggled across the sky towards one of the floating specks. Its head split open exposing a row of razor-sharp teeth, which ripped the speck to pieces. Then, as if they were prey, one by one the tendrils of cloud were hunted and consumed. It changed again, transforming into a vast cone of sand hanging motionless, like a brown stain in the night sky.

A menacing skeletal-head emerged from the apex of the cone. It bulged out over the long tail of sand – massive – taller and wider even than the twin towers guarding the portcullis; its empty eye sockets filled with swirling sand that glowed with a green light.

'Bonticas Sebola. **Omur lassint halisto.'**

The words twisted and turned in Jack's head, flipping over and over, like a Rubric cube, until they made sense.

'Arise Sebola! None must pass.'

The monster's roared and a thick funnel of loose sand spurted high into the air, blasted out as if from the throat of an open crater. Jack watched, too scared even to breathe. The face faded away into cloud, the sand-shape quickly disintegrating, crumbling to the desert floor; the wind vanishing as quickly as it had arisen.

Mendorun lowered his arms. Turning, he retraced his steps and was soon lost to view, leaving a deep silence.

'Right, let's go.'

Jack slid back through the opening into the shadow of the columns, aware there was no longer any need to set guards, the courtyard dark and empty. Even the moon, cowed by the evil in the fortress, had hidden behind a cloud. Silently, the four shadows slipped through the colonnade into the protection of the buttress of rock; Khan already stretching his hands towards the lock.

'Not yet.' Jack whispered. Stripping off the square of cotton cloth he used as a head-wrap, he scrumpled it round the bolts to muffle the noise. As the second one cleared, he held the soft cloth against the lock – beckoning Khan to open it.

The air between Khan's hands and the lock began to vibrate, becoming opaque, almost white in colour, as if Khan's fingers had created a visible pathway – like waves of heat from an electric fire when switched on in a cold room. There was the faintest of clicks and Khan pulled the gate towards them.

Abu and Shahi, believing their ordeal to be over, dashed joyously through. Angrily, Jack yanked them into the shelter of the wall. Flicking a glance upwards, he was relieved to find no angry guards glaring down at them.

'What do you think you're doing?' he stormed.

'Are we not safe yet, sir?' Abu peered up at him, his body quivering.

Jack shook his head. 'Not yet. See those lights?' In the far distance, faint pinpricks of light stood out against the dark landscape. 'That's where the town is.'

'Is that where we have to go, sir?' said Abu.

'But not on foot,' Shahi said. 'When they brought us, we came in a cart. It took many hours.'

'We haven't got a cart, so we walk. Khan,' Jack tugged at the gate, pulling it shut. 'Can you lock it again?'

''Ow do I do that, Jack? There's no key'ole on the outside.'

'Through the door, it might fool them for a minute or two anyway.'

The wood of the door was heavy and solid, designed to withstand any amount of battering. The blood vanished from Khan's straining fingers, with the force of his concentration, leaving them as white as his face.

Jack's words, *never mind, leave it,* remained unsaid as the lock clicked into place. 'That was stupendous, thanks Khan,' he slapped him on the back. 'But that's the easy bit.'

'Easy! You try it. I feel like I just run a race.'

'No, listen, I didn't mean that,' said Jack. He twined the black cord round his head, fastening his head-wrap in place. Jacob had told him how, in the olden days, the thick bands were used to hobble camels at night and prevent them from straying. 'When I was at the window Mendorun came into the courtyard. Remember, I told you he was bad?' Khan nodded. 'He seems to have conjured up some sort of monster made of sand, to stop us escaping the fortress.'

Khan's eyes opened wide staring at him.

'Mendorun is one-hundred-percent positive no one can get past it,' Jack continued. 'That's why he hasn't left any guards on the ramparts. He's sent them to search the underground tunnels.'

'So, if no one can get frou, what about us?'

'I'm pretty sure I can do it. I met up with something a bit like it before. The trick is not to think about anything.'

'Got ye, but what about them?' Khan stared meaningfully at Abou and Shahi, who were gazing out across the desert as if they expected a number-twenty-two bus to come along any minute.

A feeling of utter-helplessly overtook Jack. 'If I warn them of trouble ahead, they'll give up and wait to be recaptured. But *I'm determined to get through* and if you help me, we'll get the kids through.'

'I can't do that prayin' stuff.'

'Nor me. Best plan is to fix your eyes on the horizon and keep them there.'

'I 'ope ye're really kiddin', Jack.'

Jack was surprised to hear a note of anxiety creep into Khan's voice. His previous calm had bothered him tremendously and he felt almost pleased. Although now was not the time. If they didn't make it through, he'd have to go on alone and contact Jacob. Only Khan would never accept that without a fight.

'So do I.' He squared his shoulders. 'Let's go.' He grasped the hands of the two boys. 'Khan, you hold Abu's other hand.'

'But I can be seen,' he protested.

'It's a risk, I know, but this way you can look after Abu and I'll take Shahi.'

The main entrance to the fortress was not visible from the small gate, which had been built into the far edge of the ramparts. Shielded from unwelcome eyes by a curtain of rock, the only clue to its existence lay in a faint line of footprints leading up to it. Below the walls, the ground fell away steeply petering out into a rough track. There, a dense chain of standing stones formed yet another obstacle for anyone unwise enough to lay siege to the fortress; their elongated shape too regular both in height and width to be a natural occurrence. Jack had not noticed them on the journey in, but then he had felt too miserable and dispirited to see anything.

Continually peering over his shoulder, to make sure they'd not been spotted, he led them away from the fortress walls into the maze of rocks; conscious that every step they took was one closer to freedom and one closer to the sand monster.

He didn't have long to wait. It struck, leaving Shahi convulsed in a writhing heap on the ground.

Chapter Thirteen

The Wall of Fire

Jack shouted out, forgetting he could be heard. 'Get back in the stones, quick.' He yanked Shahi to his feet. 'What was it?' He put an arm round his shoulders.

'Fire,' the boy whimpered. 'I'm burned.'

'No, you're not,' Jack said firmly. '*You're absolute fine.* Look at your shirt … nothing on it.' He called over his shoulder. 'What about you, Abou?'

'I saw it too,' the boy said. 'But it didn't reach me.'

'And you, Khan?'

Khan met Jack's anxious gaze calmly. 'I'm OK, Jack. Like Abu said, it didn't get to me.'

If only the two youngsters could be like Khan. How could they ever succeed if, at the first step, one of them was beaten to the ground?

'It's OK, Shahi, we'll go together.'

The boy, ashen faced and terrified, stared at him blank-faced.

'Shahi, it isn't real. Cross my heart.' Jack spoke slowly, instinct convincing him he was right. But only if you believed it was an illusion would it stay that way. But how could he convince a frightened child?

'I promise you, there's nothing there.' He stared out over the desert landscape, a soft wind blowing among the hummocks of dry grass. 'No fire – nothing. *It was all your imagination.*' He clutched Shahi's hand in a fierce grip. The boy tugged at it trying to get away. 'Do you want to be captured again?'

91

The terrified boy shook his head, his eyes pleading.

'Then we go through the fire. Hang on to my hand and *don't let go.*'

Jack made up his mind. 'Khan, I'll take Shahi through first. I'll come back for you.' He hustled the two boys deep into the shadow of the rock. 'I'll be back.'

'You …'

'You've got my camel, Khan. Keep him safe or there'll be another fight,' Jack said. He kept his tone light on purpose. Khan grinned crookedly.

Before they had even gone a dozen steps, the air burst into flames around them, the leather straps on Jack's sandals beginning to smoulder in the heat. He tried to wipe the thought from his mind, ignoring the pain in his feet; but it proved impossible. It was like walking on red-hot coals.

Shahi yanked his hand free and fell to the ground clutching his head. 'My hair, it's on fire!' he screamed.

Jack shouted but the boy ignored him, curled tightly in a ball moaning. Ignoring his cries of pain, Jack hoisted him up on his shoulder in a fireman's lift.

'Pray, Shahi, pray,' he bellowed into the noise of the crackling flames.

He wasn't heavy, not as heavy as some of the lads Jack had carried when larking about. Except he wasn't fooling around now, and even the light weight of the boy took all his effort, all his concentration. He moved slowly to avoid stumbling, the exertion leaving him weakened to the suggestion of the fire. Dense smoke poured down on him making him cough, his eyes streaming. Mesmerised, he slowed to a crawl watching his sandals blacken in the heat, the leather curling up like pieces of burnt paper. He shuddered as a searing blast of heat struck his eyeballs. Shutting his eyes tightly, he set one foot in front of the other – grimly determined not to give in.

All at once, the roar of the fire vanished and it became quiet. Cautiously, he opened his eyes, feeling sand under his feet – his sandals intact, his tunic unburned. Relieved, he lowered Shahi gently to the ground but he didn't move. Frightened, Jack checked for a pulse hearing a fast, thread-like beat. Shahi was alive but unconscious.

Jacob, he called silently into the night air, *where are you?* There was no reply.

Lifting Shahi carefully, he carried him to safety under a steep ridge of sand and shrub. He had never dealt with an unconscious boy before. No one ever got badly hurt at football. Besides, there were loads of adults about to help. All Jack remembered, from the first-aid class he took as part of the coaching programme, was that the casualty would need water when he regained consciousness. And they had none. The oasis in Asfah was miles away. It also meant heading north-west, entirely the opposite direction from where Jacob would be waiting.

Jack straightened his shoulders. He would make that decision if he got the others through. *When he got them through*, he corrected himself hastily.

Turning his back on the unconscious boy, he plunged into the burning wall. His tunic instantly burst into flames, his hands blistering. Transfixed, he watched the skin bubble like a saucepan of milk. With a jolt, he caught himself up, forcing his legs into movement, shuffling forwards like an old man – all the while pushing himself deeper into the fiery furnace. Wrapping his hands over his eyes, to blank out the sight of the fire, he recited numbers, counting aloud. Feeling the pain in his feet subside, he redoubled his efforts.

'Seventy-one, seventy-two, seventy-three,' he shouted loudly and defiantly into the burning furnace; taking one step, then another and another …

Cool air brushed his cheek. He shut his eyes tight, feeling tears leak from the corners. He was through, he had made it! He sighed thankfully, wishing he could fall down on the ground and go to sleep. But he couldn't and, in a minute, he had to do it all over again.

The two boys were still there under the rock; the fortress quiet as if sleeping. Surprised, he realised time had been an illusion like the flames.

'Strewf, yew was quick,' said Khan, confirming his thoughts.

'Yeah, I wish. But it's no good wishing I didn't have to do it again, I've got to. Come on, Khan. And, remember, whatever happens keep your eyes on the horizon and don't think about it.'

He grabbed Abu's hand, flinching as the heat struck him again. If this was what it was like for him, when he had done it twice already, whatever must Khan and Abu be facing.

He knew instantly, when a volcano erupted in front of them. Lava poured down its steep slope, engulfing everything in its path. Abu screamed, pummelling Jack with his fist in a desperate attempt to break free. He held on grimly, pulling the boy deeper into the maelstrom. His shoes burst into flame, his feet ankle-deep in the molten lava. He tried to move his head to check how Khan was faring, but couldn't because his neck appeared to have melted, the vertebrae fusing together, his face fixed and staring straight ahead. His hair was alight too but he could do nothing about that, either. Abu screamed and screamed again, pulling against Jack's arms, desperate to escape the molten red of the lava flow.

Abu wasn't going to make it, he'd given up.

'*Well, I haven't,*' Jack shouted rebelliously. Using all the strength he had left, he picked the boy up, clasping him round the waist like a battering ram.

Jack couldn't think of Khan, it was all he could do to hang on to Abu, who was kicking and screaming. Khan had to make it on his own. He tried to clear his mind, to count his steps as he had done before, but found Abu's frantic attempts to escape thwarting him. The heat seared his throat and he dragged in breath after painful breath. It would be so much easier if he ceased breathing altogether. *No! He must go on!* With his last ounce of strength, Jack flung the boy forward and out of the stifling heat on to the desert floor; he and Khan collapsing on the ground beside him.

For how long they sat there, Jack had no clue. His throat felt dry and scratchy, and he guessed the others were desperate for water like him. After a while, he sat up. Khan was busily examining every inch of himself. He raised his head staring out over the desert.

'We safe, d'ye think?'

Jack gazed up at the stars twinkling overhead. In the distance the lights of the town shone bravely, the air fresh and cool.

'We should be till dawn,' he whispered hoarsely. 'But I haven't a clue how we can go any further.' He stared at Shahi, his body as rigid as a statue carved from bronze, and the hysterical Abu. 'We can't carry them, and they can't walk.'

Despairing, he covered his face with his hands resting it on his knees. Something touched him on the shoulder, nuzzling into his neck. Startled, he leapt to his feet. Gazing at him mournfully, his saddlebags full of food and water, was a camel.

'Betsy!' He flung his arms round the animal's neck sobbing, 'Jacob did send you.' Burying his face in the wool coat, he pretended to investigate the saddlebags.

'Khan, we got water.' He sniffed the tears back, rubbing his eyes. 'There's dates and bread here, too, and milk.'

Jack ran across to Abu, helping the boy to drink. 'Here, give some to Shahi.'

Shahi stirred, drinking thirstily. After a few minutes he sat up on his own, clinging tenaciously to his friend, his eyes withdrawn with pain. Khan, carrying bread, dates and honey cakes, offered the boys something to eat but neither accepted.

When he saw the little cakes, Jack felt so relieved he almost smiled, aware it was Jacob's way of saying *he'd done the best he could*. Breaking a piece off, he chewed it slowly. Never, in the whole of his life had he tasted anything so scrumptious.

'Jack,' said Khan, munching on a date. 'Thanks. We wouldn't 'ave made it wivout ye. An' you was right. I'm sorry. Ye can 'ave the camel back, I don't need it.' Removing the length of fabric from around his waist, he passed the precious bundle over.

'No sweat,' Jack got to his feet. 'Help me lift the prayer-mutterers into the saddle. Betsy, old boy, you've got to take us to Jacob. Understand?'

Betsy shook his head, accepting the heavy load with resignation, allowing the two boys to climb up. Then, with Jack in front and Khan behind, holding the two youngsters safely between them, the camel turned its back on the fortress and headed for the distant mountains.

Chapter Fourteen

Pursuit

Betsy trotted softly along his own pathway, the combined weight of the four boys slowing him down to a plodding gait. Gradually, the lights of the town vanished into the distance and, as each minute passed, Jack found himself relaxing a little, aware that any pursuit was likely to be miles away.

No one spoke; Jack and Khan content to sit quietly, breathing the pure night air, and recovering from their terrifying ordeal. From time to time, Khan leaned forward to offer water, but neither of the two small boys seemed to notice his gesture. Abu, his screaming hysteria ended, had relapsed into a stupor while Shahi, his eyes withdrawn, gazed inwards at a nightmare so horrific, it refused to leave the boy's mind.

They had travelled many miles before Jack realised that the night had almost ended, the stars already beginning to fade. If he had followed his instincts and headed for Asfah, they would have reached there by now. He remembered the guards bursting into the tent. No, not even the town was safe. That, too, was controlled by Mendorun's men.

'Betsy, look at the sky.' The camel's ears pricked up to show he was listening, the sound of the bells on his harness breaking the stillness of the air. 'At this speed we can't reach Jacob – but if you go on without us, can you make it?' The camel's head dipped in acknowledgement, its harness ringing out in affirmation.

Jack stared about him, casting around for shelter. The lower slopes were festooned with boulders, the mountain spewing out rock whenever the ground trembled, as it often did in the heat of the summer. Above them, unseen except as a solid outline against the night sky, were cliffs and escarpments, ravines and gullies, too steep for anything but the nimble feet of a goat or the sharp claws of a bird of prey.

'Why are we stoppin', we there yet?' The suspicious tones of Khan's voice broke the silence.

'Get Abu and Shahi off. Betsy's going for help.'

Khan leapt to the ground, leaving Jack to drag the comatose Abu out of the saddle. Seizing the saddlebags, Khan helped lift Shahi, the boy collapsing in a heap.

'I 'ope ye know what ye're doin',' Khan said, watching the camel disappear from sight.

'We wouldn't have made it to the cave before dawn,' Jack croaked, his throat dry even after drinking loads. He felt too exhausted to explain that Betsy, like the carving he carried strapped to his waist, would become a block of wood the moment the sun hit the sky. 'At worst we wait here till nightfall and move on as soon as it's dark.'

Instantly, Mendorun's words sprang into his head starting a relentless tattoo, *Sun-set Sun-set Sun-set.* Impatiently, he swept them aside, only to replace them with another voice – his own. *We can't stay here, we have to reach the palace by sunset otherwise they'll all be dead.* But there was no point sharing it with Khan, things were quite bad enough as it was.

'We need shelter.' Khan inspected the rock-strewn ground closely. 'Over there.'

A large fall of rock lay close by, where an avalanche had brought it hurtling down the mountainside, the roots of upended trees poking through the earth like the legs of giant spiders.

'Wait 'ere I'll check.'

Khan picked his way carefully over the moonlit track quickly vanishing from view. After a couple of minutes he reappeared.

'There's a sort'a gap round the back.' He clambered back down the loose stones towards them. 'We'll be safe there.'

'OK! Put Shahi on to my back, I'll carry him.'

Khan pulled Shahi to his feet. Despite his reassuring words, the boy resisted struggling wildly. Impatiently, Khan picked him up, manhandling him onto Jack's back.

'Shahi, we're only trying to help,' Jack staggered under the boy's weight. 'Put your arms round my neck,' he ordered, linking his hands behind him for support.

Taking a deep breath, he set his foot at the rock slope, Khan by his side. It was not far, about fifty metres or so, but it could have been miles Jack felt so tired and weak. A pebble splintered under the sole of his sandals and his ankle twisted. Khan grabbed his arm to stop him falling. Then, helping to support Shahi's weight, the two boys crawled up the slope stumbling into the alcove. Lifting Shahi down, Khan dumped the saddlebags next to him, before following Jack down the slope. Five minutes later, all four of them were safe behind the rock fall, Jack and Khan carrying the inert Abu between them.

Patiently, Khan offered both boys a drink, finally persuading Shahi to eat some dates, the boy refusing to lift his eyes from the ground.

Jack stared up at the clear patch of navy sky directly above them. 'We're going to need somewhere better than this, we can be seen from the air.'

'Does it matter?' Khan said, chewing on a hunk of bread.

'You've forgotten the crows. If they discover we've gone, they'll send the birds.'

'OK, then. Leave it te me.'

Taking his bread with him, Khan chased off, his bare feet making no sound on the solid ground. Despite his anxiety Jack's eyes began to close and, worn out, he dozed. A touch on his arm woke him and he jumped, starting up.

'I was asleep, sorry.'

'No need, mate. I found a cave. Dawn's comin' up.'

It was. Jack could already make out the particulars of Khan's face in the paling of the night sky. 'It's a bit of a climb though and it'll be tough fer 'em 'cos they can't 'elp us.'

'Then we don't go unless we have to.'

'Ye sure, Jack?'

Jack shrugged. 'Any chance of getting Abu on his feet?' Khan glanced down at the crumpled heap on the ground and shook his head. 'Can you carry him, I can't.' Khan shook his head again. 'Then we have no choice, we stay here.'

They dozed uneasily, as the sun rose into yet another cloudless day, waking at the same time. No sound had disturbed them, everything calm and peaceful in the morning light. They must have slept a couple of hours but Jack still felt dreadful. He passed the water to Khan before taking some himself.

Munching a small honey cake, he got to his feet studying the landscape of sand and shrub, leaving Khan to persuade the two boys to drink some water. Only Abu accepted, drinking a mouthful or two before relapsing into his catatonic state, his eyes glazed and unseeing. Shahi sat by his side, Abu's hand clasped in his, intently studying the stones and pebbles beneath his feet. He was silent, not even reciting prayers as he had done from the moment they'd been captured.

It was a peaceful scene in which nothing moved. Patchy clumps of greenery, mainly spiky cactus and rock plants that felt at home in the stony wilderness, basked in the glow of the early-morning light. Jack stared up at the sun, guessing it to be about seven o'clock. Still low, it had not yet gathered itself into a remorseless ball of burning heat that would gradually overwhelm everything living. Satisfied, he was about to sit down again when, out of the corner of his eye, he spotted the circling black dot.

'Khan, they've sent one of the birds,' he shouted out in panic. 'Oh, why the hell didn't we move while we had the chance.'

'No, good beatin' yerself up, Jack.' Khan peered back over the sandy desert, evidently undisturbed by the news. 'We tried, remember?'

Jack did. But he couldn't forgive himself. He knew better than anyone the danger they faced. Once the sun rose high enough, it would bleach out every shadow, highlighting every moving silhouette into bold relief.

'We'd better shift Abu first,' he lifted the boy by his shoulders. 'He's the most difficult, 'cos he can't help.'

Taking his legs, as he had done before, Khan led the way up the slope. Noise didn't matter, as loose stones broke under their feet rolling down into the rock fall, but movement did – the boys keeping as low as possible. They weren't any longer bothered about the white of their tunics giving them away. They were so filthy, they were hardly distinguishable from the sand and stone beneath their feet. Gently lowering Abu to the ground, Khan shinned up the wall onto a narrow ledge. Leaning back down, he stretched out his arms ready to pull Abu up.

'Lift your arms,' Jack said, hoisting Abu onto his feet. He took no notice, his head dropped forward on his chest.

'Pick 'im up Jack,' Khan called impatiently.

'I *can't*, he's too heavy.' Defeated, Jack gazed miserably at the silent boy. 'This was a stupid idea,' he stormed. 'We'll never get him up there. We'll have to take him back and risk being spotted.'

'Gimme ye're 'ead-wrap, quick.'

Jack passed it up. Tearing off the string from round his head, Khan tied the two pieces of cloth together.

'If I 'old this end, can ye put it round Abu?'

Catching the makeshift rope, Jack passed it under the boy's thin shoulders, fastening it round his chest. It stretched tight, lifting Abu up on his tiptoes. The boy ignored it. His eyes remained closed, his body heavy and unable to help.

With Jack supporting his weight, Khan hauled on the improvised rope; the boy's knees scraping painfully over the rock face. It had to have hurt but Abu didn't appear to notice, totally oblivious to what was happening. Jack steadied him by his hips, then his legs – conscious of a desperate need to hurry.

'Got 'im,' Khan called triumphantly, hauling Abu onto the ledge.

Jack dug his right toe into a crack and pulled himself up, finding it easy to climb the broken face. He hauled himself over the edge, noticing Khan had already removed the sling. Stepping over the unconscious boy, they managed to drag him into the cave. Twilight beckoned, offering a feeling of safety. Except, it was false feeling. They still had to get Shahi up the sun-filled slope; all the time conscious of the black menace soaring overhead, with its superbly magnified eyesight that could spot a mouse moving on the ground.

Climbing down was easy. Now they had done it once, the vertical wall posed no problem. Reckless of the loose stones, Jack and Khan slithered fast down the slope towards the sheltering rocks. Every second was precious and they needed to hurry, before the bird moved its search towards them.

Khan reached the alcove first. He shook Shahi's shoulder to rouse him.

'Come on, mate, climb up on Jack's back, like ye did before. We got Abu safe already. Come on.'

Slinging the saddlebags over his shoulder, he grasped Shahi by the hand. The boy struggled and broke free, heading for the slope below.

'Shahi, come back, not that way,' yelled Jack diving after him.

He seized his arm but Shahi pulled away in panic, his eyes riveted to the ground.

'It's this way, Shahi.' Jack forced himself to speak quietly, so as not to frighten the already terrified boy further. 'We've found a cave and Abu, your friend, is there. Come on, you can help me look after him.'

A faint squawk broke the silence. Jack flinched as if he'd been struck. High above them, only a speck but coming closer, descending towards the lower levels of the air even as he watched, was the crow.

'GO, KHAN, GO. LEAVE EVERYTHING. GET TO THE CAVE. SHAHI, RUN!'

Pulling the reluctant boy after him, Jack tore up the shale slope, slipping and sliding, uncaring if he hurt his ankle because, at any second, he expected to feel talons in his back.

'Shahi, can you climb?' The rock ledge loomed above them. The boy shook his head. 'OK, I'll help you.' Jack struggled to slip the make-shift rope over Shahi's head, his hands shaking violently.

The boy flung up his arms, knocking the sling away.

Jack swore. *Jeez! Of all the times to be difficult.* 'Khan,' he shouted. 'Can you help?' There was no reply. He glanced over his shoulder but Khan was nowhere in sight.

'Blast!' he swore, attempting once again to get the loop over Shahi's head – all the time muttering calming words.

The silence of the morning was broken by a series of thumps, as if someone was wielding a stone hammer. It continued for a minute or two, followed by a tearing and ripping sound. Khan reappeared carrying a branch he'd managed to break off from one of the trees, torn up by the landslip.

'You go, Jack. 'E'll move for you.'

'But you can't!' Jack gasped, guessing what Khan was planning to do.

'Yeah, I can. Street fightin's my game. But 'urry, I won't be able to 'old that bastard crow fer long.'

The steady drone of wings filled the silence of the morning. Winding the rope round Shahi's waist, Jack hurriedly looped the other end around his own, tying it firmly. The boy, taking no further interest, allowed Jack to place his hands and feet in the first of the cracks. Giving him a shove from behind, Jack forced him off the ground before pulling himself up. Then, sharing his own weight between the fingers of his right-hand and his two feet, he leaned over and hauled him up another step, the cotton rope grasping Shahi tightly. Wishing he had eyes in the back of his head, he jammed the boy's fingers into a crack, holding them there until he felt them grip the stone, Shahi automatically bringing his feet up. He continued to edge upwards, the rope hampering his movements.

'Take that ye friggin' monster.'

The branch struck the bird's face, its intention to pierce Khan's chest with the speed of its dive thwarted. Failing, it squawked loudly and lashed out with its fluttering wings. Khan struck again, using the branch as a spear. He twisted it round in his hands, turning it into a stave to ward off the beak, pecking away at his face like a flurry of right-handed jabs from a boxer's glove.

Spread-eagled against the rock, Jack searched for the next handhold, listening panic-stricken to the sounds of the fracas below. But there was nothing he could do – not until he had Shahi safe. He heard the snapping of the bird's beak and the scratching of its gigantic talons on the stone, conscious they were attacking any part of Khan within reach.

'Hurry Shahi,' he urged, wanting to scream at the boy for being so slow. 'We're nearly there – two more steps.'

He crawled onto the ledge, grazing his knees on the rough surface. Leaning down, he grabbed the boy's hand, which was wandering aimlessly between the cracks as if he was on a Sunday school outing, not fleeing a virago of black feathers with murder on its mind. In the background, he caught the angry sound of bunched fists hitting their feathery-target and a piercing yell from Khan, as he was knocked off his feet.

Safe on the ledge, Shahi looked vaguely about him, not the slightest bit concerned about what was happening below. Jack fumbled with the knot at his waist, angry the boy couldn't even help with that. Then, heedless of whether he was hurting him, pushed him into the cave.

'Stay with Abu,' he shouted and ran out to help Khan, swinging the knotted rope round his head.

He was too late!

Khan, already off balance, bravely swung the branch as the bird's head butted him in the shoulder. It knocked him backwards and he struck his head on the rock-hard ground, falling senseless. The crow stretched its black wings. It crowed triumphantly, undulating its feathers, as it lifted its head for the coup de grace.

'YOU CAN'T,' screamed Jack, hurtling down the rock face. 'KHAN!'

Chapter Fifteen

Rescued

A tumultuous roar filled the air, blasting against Jack's ear drums. A pale tawny shape leapt from the rock onto the back of the jubilant bird. It squawked and lashed out, but the animal, its head buried in the bird's neck, held fast. The huge bird shook itself violently in an attempt to escape.

Jack pulled Khan to his feet dragging him towards the wall. Disorientated, Khan struggled to reach the cracks. Aware his friend was badly injured Jack went ahead, stretching out an arm to help him up. Not daring to look back, they scrambled up the cliff face, falling exhausted onto the flat ledge. Then, stumbling with weariness, they crawled into the shelter of the cave where they sat trembling; the blood from Khan's wounds dripping onto Jack's tunic.

Roars and screams of pain filled the air, followed by silence. Jack gazed at Khan's face white and strained, mirroring his own, neither boy daring to speak.

A shadow fell across the sunlit ledge, followed by the tawny shape of a lion. It searched deep into the cave, its eyes roaming the depths of the gloom. Sprawling full length, it began to lick the tears and scratches on its paws and front legs.

Jack and Khan stared at the huge beast. Subsonic rumblings, from the back of the animal's throat, filled the air; the two boys not daring to move a muscle in case it saw them. Suddenly Shahi whimpered. The lion paused staring at the little group of boys, the two nearest clutching each other in terror. It studied them gravely for a second before looking away again, continuing its efforts to clean its ripped paw.

Jack felt so tired he couldn't think. They'd really had it this time. His luck had finally run out. Now, there were no options. They were stuck in a cave with a lion blocking the exit and no one to rescue them. All they could do was remain still and pray the animal wasn't hungry, and would go away. It hadn't attacked them yet, but then they hadn't moved.

His head jerked up in astonishment as he felt Khan loose his hand. Shocked rigid, he watched him climb slowly to his feet.

'No!' he mouthed, shaking his head.

Khan patted the air with his hand, as if to say *be quiet*. Limping badly, he edged towards the front of the cave. The lion took no notice allowing Khan to approach closely; the tawny eyes studying the figure as if assessing exactly what the boy was worth in terms of food.

Jack held his breath, almost dying with shock as he saw Khan stretch out his hand. He almost did die with shock when the huge beast bent its head and licked Khan's hand, its tongue rasping noisily over the skin.

'Khan?' he asked in bewilderment.

'It's OK. 'E won't 'arm us,' Khan said stroking the animal's head. ''E came 'ere to save us.'

'Save us?' Jack echoed. Daylight dawned. 'You're one of Jacob animals, aren't you?' he shouted excitedly. 'Can you speak?' The great mane rustled. 'Is Jacob coming?' The lion inclined its head, calmly licking at its paw.

Jack broke into hysterical laugher. 'Do you know what that means, Khan? *We've done it! We're actually safe!*

***

Two circling specs kept the boys company, as they sat in the cave opening behind the sleeping form of the lion; although the scavenging vultures, anticipating an unexpected feast, kept their distance out of respect for its tawny shape.

Jack too exhausted to sleep watched them, aware they would have alerted Mendorun to their whereabouts but somehow quietly confident that Jacob would reach them first.

He did. A rattle of stones on the path below heralded the arrival of the camel, with the irascible shape of the donkey trotting behind. A minute later Jacob's head appeared over the rock edge.

'As if I am not too old to climb cliffs,' he panted. His eyes flashed round the cave noting everything. 'The Gods be prais-ed, we were in time, my Lord Burnside.'

'We're all right now, Jacob, but we weren't till your friend arrived.'

Jacob glanced at Khan sitting quietly by Jack's side, his hand on the lion's mane.

'This is Khan,' said Jack. 'He saved our lives when the crow attacked.'

'You saved me first, Jack; ye got us frou the fire, remember.'

'But *you, Khan* …'

'*Hsst! Hsst!* There will be time for this litany of compliments later.' Jacob raised his arm like a policeman arresting the flow of words. 'We have more important matters to attend to, my Lord Burnside. You and your friend, Khan, can spend as many days as you wish eulogising each other, once you are safe.'

Jack smiled wearily finding it difficult, however tired he was, to be serious in the face of Jacob's extraordinary manner of conversation.

'You can get us out of here though, before Mendorun arrives?' he said.

'Yes, yes, yes! But there are questions to ask first. The camel?'

'I've got him, Jacob.' Jack tugged at the cloth containing the wooden animal, which was still wrapped round his waist. He handed the silent carving to Jacob. 'But I think Mendorun got to him first.'

'How is that possible?' said Jacob, stroking the soft wooden sides of the statue. 'As always, Lord Burnside, you succeed but at grave cost, I fear.' He studied the two boys crouched in the corner, completely oblivious to the newcomers in the cave. '*Tell me, tell me all.*'

Jack shook his head. 'No! Explanations can wait. There's something far more important I need to tell you first. I was that worried … in case we didn't make it in time and …' Jack's voice cracked.

The sorcerer's eyes flashed, glinting under his eyebrows, his arms quietly nursing the statue of the little camel. 'I am here now, my Lord, so tell me what concerns you.'

'I overheard Mendorun and Saladin talking.'

'*Saladin* – that damn-ed dog! He is still alive?'

Jack nodded wearily, remembering Jacob's assurance that Saladin would be long gone. How wrong they have been. 'Saladin was asking what Mendorun had done about Prince Salah. He told him the bird would drop poison into the well at sunset tomorrow … I mean, today.'

'There is more?'

'Yes. He said you'd be killed, too. And when Saladin asked if you could stop it, he said, "*No one could stop it now the sorcerer's familiar was destroyed.*" There was something about the birds. "*The birds gave him superb power.*" That's not right. "*Supreme power*", whatever that is – and you being "*a rudderless ship in a storm?*" And Mendorun said he was the storm.'

Jacob was silent, simply turning the wooden animal round and round in his hands.

'Can you stop him, Jacob?' asked Jack, hardly daring to put his thoughts into speech, for fear of the answer.

Under the deeply-frowning brows, hawk-like eyes gleamed at Jack. 'Indeed I must, if we are to live our lives in safety.'

'But how? You can't even see through Mendorun's aura?' Jack blurted out. 'We were stuck in that hell hole and you didn't come.'

'There was nothing I could do,' Jacob replied, his voice stern. 'There is no sorcerer alive that can penetrate the blackness with which Mendorun surrounds himself. At first, this power was but a pool surrounding him as he walked. As he has grown strong, so it too has grown and its circumference extends many miles. But I had seen you in the future, and I felt certain you would be safe. The moment you were free of the circle and climbing the rocks to the cave, I sent our friend here,' he indicated the sleeping lion. 'And I came myself.' Jacob's voice trailed away. 'But, I do not understand, I had sent the camel to bring you out of the fortress. Why did it fail?'

'That was Mendorun's doing, too.' Abruptly Jack's anger died, replaced with a feeling of shame. None of this was Jacob's fault. If it was anyone's it was his; stupidly shouting out in a town already traumatised by fear. 'He created a wall of fire. Even Betsy couldn't have got through that.'

'And yet, my Lord Burnside, you got through.'

'I guess, but I don't know what it's done to Khan, he won't say.' Jack flashed a grin at the silent boy. 'And look at those two – they haven't spoken since.'

Jacob rose swiftly to his feet, his shoulders once again hunched, his hands revolving at speed, his eyes hidden.

'Come – if what you say is true, my Lord Burnside, there is indeed no time to be lost. We must go to the palace, and without delay.'

Chapter Sixteen

The Kingdom of Sudana

An extraordinary, and very weary, party emerged onto the sun-baked slopes of the hills surrounding the palace. Jacob led the camel with the two sick boys on its back. Khan, Jack and the lion – all three limping – walked by its side; Khan and Jack steadying the youngsters as they swayed and lurched with the camel's awkward gait. The donkey, eyeing the lion with considerable distaste, brought up the rear. Jacob, worried about Khan's wounds, had suggested he ride the donkey but he had stubbornly refused, saying if Jack was going to walk then so was he.

The fields surrounding the palace were busy. Work started before six whilst the day was still cool, finishing before midday when the sun became a blistering ball of fire in the sky. Recognising Jacob, men ran to fetch a cart carefully transferring the two youngsters into it.

Before long, the sparkling towers and domes of the palace loomed over them. Guards, on the battlements, peered curiously down at the party making its way towards the great iron gates, which were open but well guarded.

'Ye said ye 'ad powerful friends, Jack, but wow,' exclaimed Khan as they passed through the stone arch and across the outer courtyard, under the watchful eye of men guarding the wall above them.

Up close the palace resembled a fairy-tale theme park, with towers of green set amidst apricot-coloured walls. But its appearance was deceptive. Its walls were patrolled night and day by heavily armed guards and arrows could be launched from the towers, killing anyone unwise enough to attempt to breach the wall. Even if they made it across the courtyard, a second fortified wall, guarded by a vast bronze gate, stood in their way. Only if they got through that would they reach the palace proper, with its gardens and fountains, and halls with their domed roofs.

A small figure waited for them – a lock of black hair falling over his eyes.

'Saleem!' yelled Jack, rushing over to hug his friend.

'Hell's Bloody Bells, Jack.' Saleem exclaimed in English. He pushed his friend away, holding him at arm's length. 'I might be glad to see you, but not that glad, you're filthy!'

'This is Khan.' Jack said, reverting to Arabic. He dragged the reluctant boy forward. 'He's a friend.'

'You're hurt,' Saleem said, noticing Khan's arm where the bird had torn it open. 'So you can speak *my* language now, can you, Jack? You've definitely been having adventures, and without me; that's not fair.'

'I'd 'ave swapped,' muttered Khan, half-smiling at the Prince.

'And you may yet get your wish, my Lord Saleem. For this is not over. But for now, my Lord Burnside and the boy, Khan, must sleep.'

'And wash,' said Saleem.

'And eat,' added Jack, absolutely famished. 'But what about Abu and Shahi *and that other matter, Jacob?*'

'You may safely leave everything to me and sleep. Prince Saleem and I will take care of the children. I will attend to your injuries shortly, young Khan.'

'Is 'e really a prince?' whispered Khan, following Saleem through the garden of flowering trees, bright streams of water from the fountains cooling the air.

'Yes, I am,' Saleem called cheerfully, overhearing Khan's whispered words. 'But don't let that bother you, I don't.'

A grove of miniature palms, their leaves like giant fans, accompanied them along a white marble path towards the guest suite at the rear of the palace; the rooms always kept prepared for unexpected visitors.

Jacob was right. No sooner had he showered and changed his clothes, than Jack found himself dropping in his tracks and, curling up on his bed, was instantly asleep.

Sunlight streamed into his room, through the open doors to the balcony, when he finally awoke. A knock sounded on his door. It opened to reveal a grinning Iqbal, one of the servant boys, with a tray of food; Jacob following behind.

'Jacob – Iqbal – put the tray down. It's great to see you.'

The boy's mouth dropped open and he started violently, as if he had seen a ghost. The sorcerer snatched the tray before he dropped it, placing it carefully on a table.

Iqbal pointed at Jack, his fingers trembling.

'What the heck's the matter?' Jack said. 'Have I grown two heads?'

'B…b…but you speak our language, effendhi,' stuttered the boy.

'I speak … Oh help! I forgot.' He gave the boy a friendly grin. 'Sorry, Iqbal, I've been having lessons.'

The boy shot him a doubtful look. 'They are very good lessons, my Lord.'

'Yeah, Jacob taught me,' Jack said gleefully, implicating the silent figure. You'd better warn the others, so they don't get a shock.'

Iqbal tore out of the room, not sure quite whether he liked the new Jack Burnside.

'Oh bother, Jacob. It feels so natural now.'

'No harm done. By the time the boy has boasted to all his friends, he will believe he taught you the language himself.'

'That reminds me.' Jack eyes sparkled with pleasure at the sight of the tray, laden with his favourite meal of bread, honey, yoghurt and dates. 'Whatever happened to Yazim, the boy that was lost in the sandstorm?'

'Prince Saleem found him the following day wandering on the mountain.'

Jack flashed a relieved smile. 'Oh, that's great. At least that's one thing I no longer have to worry about.'

'You worry too much, my Lord Burnside. Now eat.'

'You *said* to sleep.'

'You have slept.' Forestalling all argument Jacob added, 'But a few hours only, not nearly enough, I agree. But if you do not witness the defeat of Mendorun's evil plots, you will ask so many questions I shall be forced to turn *you* into a block of wood, like the curs-ed camel.

Jack didn't reply too busy filling the gaping void in his belly. But Jacob was right, he would have asked non-stop questions but where …

'We go to the cave,' said Jacob, exactly as if Jack had spoken out loud. 'If you have finished scraping the pattern off that plate …'

'What about Khan?'

'He needs sleep to heal his wounds. Come, let us go.'

***

Jack gazed round at the familiar walls of the invisible cave, a small fire piercing the gloom. Naturally, Jacob hadn't bothered to explain how he came to create such a cave or how it was able to move from one place to another. Still, Jacob only ever half-explained anything and, only then, if forced. The only way, he could make sense of the cave, was by pretending it was the interior of the box. Once inside, you could move about.

Thoughtfully, he stepped out into the daylight, keeping a tight grip on the edge of the wall. If he lost contact, locating it again would be tricky. The afternoon sun remained high, the ground incapable of absorbing any more heat blasted into submission.

Was it really only yesterday that he'd set out from the hotel? Time had certainly been stretched to breaking point. First-thing Friday morning, the market at Jellalabar Road, followed by the invisible cave; both of them in Morocco. Then, on Friday afternoon, their spine-tingling dash through space to Asfah, followed by that horrendous few hours in the fortress.

And now … His eyes followed the line of cultivation, fields drifting down the mountain slopes towards the palace walls, its domed roofs shimmering in the sunlight. To the south-east, the fluttering crowns of palm trees pin-pointed the little town of Tigrit. He was in the kingdom of Sudana, which Jacob had kept safe for so many years. And it was only Saturday afternoon.

Jack quickly revised his timetable, realising it had been slightly ambitious. It didn't matter though; he could easily make it back by tonight or tomorrow morning at the very latest.

'You know that lion?' Ducking down, to avoid striking his head on walls he couldn't see, Jack sat down cross-legged opposite Jacob.

'Sengila?'

'Is that his name? I thought he was one of the animals you carved from wood, like Betsy. But he couldn't have been, could he? It was bright sunlight. That makes him real. So, how come he understood us?'

'Sengila possesses a rare magic. He can also speak. You must learn to listen, my Lord Burnside.'

'Listen?' Jack sounded puzzled.

'Sengila communicates using telepathy. A simple gift which you can easily acquire.'

'I think Khan can do it already.'

'It's quite possible. Be that as it may, the lion does not live with me. I sent for him after you were captured, for at that moment I had great need of him. Tell me about the boy. Where does he come from?'

'He said the streets somewhere.'

'And his family?'

'Doesn't have one. I expect he ran away from home.'

'But his name?'

Jack shifted about trying to find a comfortable spot on the rough ground. 'Told me he made it up. He's ever so strange.'

'Go on,' Jacob busied himself making the tea, as if what Jack was telling him was of little interest. Jack would have believed it too, had he not noticed Jacob's hands were no longer whirling round and round.

'When we were in the cage he was that calm. I was shaking.' Jack shook his head several times, as if to emphasise how very puzzling he had found it. 'It was odd all right. And when I challenged him, he said he could open locks.'

Jacob glanced up sharply, his eyes glinting.

'It was as weird as some of the stuff you do – and that's saying something. He just held out his hands ...' Jack mimicked the action, his fingers out rigid. 'And a sort of current, like the exhaust fumes on an airplane, shot through the air. I tell you, Jacob, what with that and me being invisible, we had a fine time.'

'You say he can open doors?'

'That's what I was telling you, if you were listening,' Jack said indignantly.

'Can he do anything else?'

'Besides fight? He's brave and fearless. He protected me from Saladin.'

Jack told the story of their escape, Jacob sitting quietly on the ground, his chin resting on his bent knee.

'And now he wishes to return to the streets of Pulah?'

'Pulah?' Jack said, astonished.

'From what you said the cart picked him up trolling the streets. There are no children in Asfah.'

'That's right, I forgot. That's what was missing – *children* – but why, Jacob?'

'Because the carts had already done their work, until the people became so frightened they sent the remaining children away.'

'So that's what Saladin meant about being promised six children. But what does Mendorun want them for?'

Jacob shrugged. 'Tell me why Khan wishes to return to Pulah?'

'Oh! That's when we hated one another,' Jack grimaced, feeling rather shamefaced. 'We argued and I hit him,' he confessed.

'You fought, whilst escaping the clutches of Mendorun? Somewhat ...'

'Stupid – childish ... I tell you what though,' he burst out. 'He may not have been to school, and he's a right pain sometimes, but if I was in a tight spot I'd rather have *him* with me than anyone, except Bud, of course.'

'And now?'

'I'd kind'a like him to stay around if he would.'

'Well, we will ask. Here.' Jacob handed him a small glass of hot tea.

Wishing it was a Coke, Jack sipped at the sweet beverage. In this country, you only had to stand still for a moment before someone made tea and expected you to drink it. Although, it did make a kind of sense. He remembered Barney's warning, when they first arrived in Rabat, to make sure they drank only bottled or boiled water.

He started up. 'Jacob, I ought to leave pretty soon. I don't want my friends getting into trouble because I'm missing.'

Jacob waved the problem away with a flutter of his fingers. 'Once that troublesome animal is back on his feet, he will take you.'

'That's great – thanks,' said Jack, instantly feeling a lot happier about life in general.

'Tell me how you found him.'

'After we got out of the cage … that's when I discovered I could go invisible. How did you manage that, Jacob? I wondered if it was something to do with that strange language.'

'Yes, my Lord Burnside, the language is exceedingly useful. Go on!'

'I knew Bud was somewhere in the fortress. You were right, I could sense he was close by. Anyhow, when Khan opened the door to this room – that's when I saw the birds. There was this huge cave …' Jack hesitated, seeing the dark walls of the cave in his mind, so dark the oil lamps made little difference. 'That's probably why Mendorun built his fortress on that spot in the first place, because it was sitting on all these caves.' He shivered. 'That man really is the devil, Jacob. Scares me to death, I can tell you.'

'There is more?'

'A section of the cave was open. I saw the night sky. And there was this golden light – like a huge floodlight staring at the ground. The birds were asleep on some wooden stands,' Jack sketched the shape in the air. 'Only a few were under the light, the rest were in shadow. I saw thirteen altogether but the lion killed one.'

'And the light?'

'Um … it was warm and round … a bit like a tube. Only it didn't spread out like light usually does. Instead, it seemed to glue the roof to the floor, like it was holding it up … only, as I told you, in one place there wasn't any roof.'

'I feared this when you were attacked by that giant crow many moons ago,' Jacob said. 'Mendorun has discovered the secret of making positive energy.'

'What's that??'

'It is similar to an electric current, Lord Burnside, except that it flows only one way. There is no negative energy to return the current to its source. A light source drives the current into the cells of an object and, provided it is living, it grows rapidly. Mendorun has simply used a normal crow and poured beams of light into it, until it is the size you encountered.'

'But what about Bud?'

'That animal! He is very different. Yet, even as ordinary wood loses its lustre if left in sunlight; so for the camel positive energy, like the sun, is also an enemy. When bombarded, the molecules on the surface of the wood react as if they have been invaded and repel the charge, by simply remaining inert. Although, after several weeks, even they would have broken down. Thanks to you, the animal was not there long enough for this to happen.'

'Jacob, there are dozens of stands,' Jack said, in a worried tone of voice.

'If so, we must expect dozens of birds. Wait here, for however much it grieves me, I must bring this loathsome animal back to life and, once again, expose myself to a barrage of insults.'

Concealed by the cumbersome silhouettes of the camel and donkey, Jack hadn't noticed the small grotto tucked into the back of the cave; tongues of rock like the teeth of a comb shielding it from view. A bolt of light shot through the cave and ripples of blue, like waves on the sea shore, danced across the wall. Startled, Jack swung round, spotting Jacob's hunched silhouette against a vivid blue background; his arms like the fronds of a palm tree in a gale. Gradually, the brilliant steam of light retracted to form a single shaft of colour, streaming down from the low roof. Placing the wooden camel in the centre, Jacob watched for a minute or two. Then, apparently satisfied, left the hidden grotto.

'Is that the negative charge?'

'Of course.' Jacob picked up his tea, joining Jack by the cave entrance. 'Hopefully by tomorrow it will have done its work. It is too much to expect that the light will have improved the animal's disposition. Watch the horizon carefully, my Lord, for the sun is beginning to slip.'

Sunset came swiftly; the sun dropping towards the horizon like a stone into water, a green flash flaring briefly before it too slipped away, allowing the pale navy of the new-born night into the sky. Nothing happened, the skies remaining clear. Jacob rose to his feet, interrupting their silent vigil, his robes rustling as he crossed the cave. He ducked under the shelf of rock into the cavity at the rear of the cave, filled with its brilliant blue light.

'Here, my Lord, come and help.' He handed Jack a wooden statue of a wildebeest. Carved in the same wood as the camel, its surface was warm and velvety. It looked wild and fierce, its horns projecting aggressively out of its forehead. 'Put them by the light, over there,' he instructed, handing him a second animal – the carving almost identical.

'What are these for?'

'I thought to bring some of the animals to life.'

'But the birds will fly over them?' Jack said in astonishment.

'Not these, my Lord Burnside, not these.'

Still not convinced, Jack reluctantly placed the small statues on the floor, taking care not to damage the intricate carving of the horns, fetching two more and then another two. Jacob followed, carrying one in each hand.

'But there's only eight! That's nowhere near enough,' Jack protested. 'There were dozens of stands.'

'Believe me these beasts are worth a bushel of crows any day.' The heavy eyebrows lifted, the hidden eyes regarding the boy for a brief second, before the sorcerer resumed his task of arranging them on the ground. 'I would advise standing well out of the way, Lord Burnside. They are somewhat ferocious and impartial as to what they trample on.'

The magic that Jack had watched, time and time again, change Bud from a wooden statue into a sneering, sarcastic camel, wove its spell around the eight pieces of wood. The shadows flared onto the wall, growing and growing, and bellows of frustrated belligerence filled the cave. Jack dived for safety behind a rock, as the wall in front of him filled to overflowing with the eight beasts. Heads butted, horns clashed angrily, hooves struck sparks as they kicked and jostled in the confined space; their eyes hysterical, the whites rimmed blood-red.

The cave filled with the rancid smell of fetid breath as the gigantic beasts tore out of the surface of the rock and flung themselves into the air beyond the cave, their screams and bellows fading as they disappeared from view.

Jack found he was gripping the rock in front of him so tightly his fingers hurt.

'I see what you mean,' he muttered, rubbing them briskly to restore the circulation. He felt as breathless as if he had run a marathon. 'I almost feel sorry for the crows now.'

Jacob clapped his hands and a camel sidled out of the shadows.

'*Betsy!*' yelled Jack, delighted to see his friend.

'I'm surprised at your pleasure, my Lord Burnside. Is this not the animal that failed miserably to reach me before dawn struck?'

'Yeah, but he saved our bacon first.' Jack grinned, patting the camel's nose.

'Come. We must hurry back to the palace. They will shortly be serving dinner.'

Chapter Seventeen

A Voice in the Night

The domed roof of the great hall bristled with light and noise as the inhabitants of the palace, ministers, clerks, and friends of the ruler, met up for dinner with their families.

Nicknamed the Rainbow Hall by Saleem, seven tents of fluted silk filled the area beneath the golden dome, the fabric so sheer lanterns glowed like fireflies dancing in the air.

Prince Salah, noticing Khan's look of amazement, explained that his people had been nomads for centuries, travelling throughout the lands of Asia. 'I built the hall in this way to remind us of our heritage,' he added.

The ruler was a gentle, courteous man, and a scholar, speaking several languages including English. Tragically, his long imprisonment had left an indelible mark and he remained thin and stooped, his hair prematurely grey. Looking at him, Jack found it impossible to believe that Saladin, with his evil treachery, could possibly be his brother.

Saleem, seated on the right of his father with Khan next to him, had chosen the purple tent, his favourite, for dinner that night. From all around, the sounds of conversation and happy laughter floated into the air, the majority of the people that lived and worked in the palace present at dinner. Only the two youngsters were missing, Jacob saying they were asleep and he didn't wish them disturbed until morning.

Jack spoke little, content to let the conversation wash over him. He felt desperately tired and – even worse – desperately nervous, worried that Jacob had under-estimated the danger they were in – the looming power of Mendorun's words still preying on his mind.

He glanced over to where the sorcerer, in robes of silk, was chatting with the ruler of the kingdom, astonished by his sudden transformation into an elegant individual with quiet hands, his back ramrod straight. It was so weird, it was unbelievable. And it was happening more and more often – and so quickly – as if one person had left the room and another had entered. One moment, it was that nervous, irritable individual with whom Jack had become so comfortable, constantly at war with hands that flew in and out of his voluminous sleeves like the space shuttle; the next, it was someone at least ten centimetres taller, with a voice as deep and still as a bottomless lake, power oozing from every pore. Only the hooded eyes remained the same.

And how many disguises were there? Like in Asfah, when the soldiers broke into their tent – the crippled old man. Jacob reminded him of a chameleon that readily absorbed colour from the leaf or twig on which it was perched. But which was real person? The Jacob he knew so well or the other one? And why? To keep him safe? If so, from whom?

Khan, overwhelmed by the splendour of his surroundings, sat silently also only replying if spoken to. He'd confided in Jack that he'd never before slept in a bed with mosquito netting or taken a shower, and the servant had had to show him how the taps worked. To put him at his ease, Saleem and Mercedes, Jacob's fourteen year-old daughter, took turns talking about the little kingdom and its people, and why they didn't have telephones or televisions, because nothing worked so close to the mountains.

'Take dinner,' Mercedes said. 'There must be sixty people in this room.' She waved her hand airily towards the other tents, each one decorated in one of the rainbow colours. 'Believe it or not, this entire dinner was cooked on an open fire.'

Khan stared in astonishment at the assortment of dishes on the small tables – all of them piping hot and so delicious, it was difficult to decide which to eat first.

On first meeting Mercedes, Khan had been rather shy of the tall girl in the beautifully coloured robe, with glittering jewels on her wrists and neck. Then Saleem explained that Mercedes only wore dresses for dinner, when she was on her best behaviour, preferring jeans most of the time. 'And if she challenges you to a fight – say no,' he had instructed.

'Trust Mercedes only to give you half a story,' Saleem broke in. 'The fire happens to be big enough to roast a whole ox, and there are huge ovens on either side. I can fit into them easily although Mercedes can't, she's too tall,' he teased. 'Plus, there's a griddle on top, for making bread.' He indicated the baskets of flat bread which had been served hot; servants running backwards and forwards to refill them as they became empty.

'I was making a point, Sally,' Mercedes smiled sweetly, nonchalantly twirling one of her curls round her finger.

Jack hid a grin. If they hadn't been at dinner, Mercedes would have stuck her tongue out at Saleem. The best of friends, they were always arguing.

'If you remember we don't have any mod cons here,' she added.

'We have electricity.' Saleem reminded her indignantly.

'Not in the palace, we don't.'

'Mercedes is quite correct,' Prince Salah said, overhearing. 'I have always preferred oil lamps.' He smiled at Khan, his serious face lighting up briefly. 'We do possess a generator but it is reserved for the guest rooms and the floodlights at the football ground.'

'Football!'

'Of course, we have an excellent team, thanks to Jack. Also my son, Saleem, is very keen. Until last season, he played with Jack in

Birmingham – that is how they met.'

After dinner, the Prince courteously wished his guests good night, suggesting the four youngsters went off to play table tennis in the games room. He left the tent, Jacob accompanying him.

'You comin', Jack?'

'Not tonight, if you don't mind. I'm heading straight for bed, I'm knackered,' Jack said, beginning to feel light-headed from lack of sleep. 'I only had a couple of hours.'

'Your loss,' said Mercedes. 'I was about to tell Khan about our lion, Adolphus. It's a great story. I mean you've never in your life seen a lion that big.' She flung out her arms describing a half-circle in the air. '*He was enormous.*'

Jack shook his head, aware he was quite likely to fall asleep standing up if he didn't get to bed soon. Waving goodnight to his friends, he wandered off round the courtyard towards the guest suite. In the warm air, the orange flowers of a Jacaranda tree floated to the ground creating a carpet for him to walk on. Far off, he heard Mercedes talking.

'Told us he came from Trafalgar Square, wherever that is.'

'It's in London.' Jack recognised Saleem's voice. 'There are four stone lions that guard Nelson's Column.'

'Who's telling this story, you or me, Sally? Anyway, he spent a few weeks in the sun with us here. Said it was good for his rheumatism. Then he disappeared again. Pops never did explain why.'

Mercedes was a prickly character – exactly like Jacob – suspicious of anything new or different, but she had obviously accepted Khan.

***

Jack shot up in bed, suddenly wide awake, convinced someone close by had spoken his name. He stared round his room; the flimsy curtains at the window swinging slightly in the breeze. He remembered opening the shutters for some much-needed air, but nothing else. Obviously, he'd fallen asleep as soon as his head had touched the pillow.

'Wake up, Jack Burnside, wake up,' the voice called. So he hadn't dreamt it. Alarmed, Jack realised that no one had spoken aloud, the sound came from inside his head.

Flinging himself out of bed, he grabbed his jeans diving headfirst into his shirt. Clutching his trainers in one hand, he ran for the door and pulled it open, cannoning into Khan.

'Did ye call me, Jack, I 'eard somefin'.'

'I think it was Sengila.' Jack headed for the stairs, Khan chasing behind him.

'Oo's that?'

'It's the lion.'

'Blimey!' Khan stopped dead halfway down the stairs. 'There ain't 'alf some weird goin's-on in this place.'

Jack laughed. 'Can't you go a bit faster, we've got to find Jacob – sometime before dawn,' he added sarcastically. 'And if you think Sengila's weird – wait a bit.'

There was no one around, the palace quietly sleeping. Silently, the two boys slipped along the pathways, wending their way through the trees and fountains of the inner courtyard, only to find the guards at the bronze gate slumped on the ground fast asleep.

'Fat lot of good you'd be,' Jack said indignantly, shaking one of the sleeping bodies awake, 'if anyone did attack.'

Leaving the two men staggering back onto their feet, he led the way towards a narrow alleyway near the kitchens, emerging in the outer courtyard. Rarely used, and then only by servants, it had once performed a great service for Jack by saving his life.

Recognising the youths as guests of the ruler, the guard patrolling that section of the wall tilted his spear in a friendly gesture. But, apart from him and the men stationed in the tall towers, whose job it was to keep a watchful eye on the land beyond the gates, there was no sign that anyone was awake.

Jack tore through the courtyard, heading for the rear of the palace. On its north-east corner, staring out across the starlit fields, was a lone figure, the lion crouched at his feet.

'Ah, my Lord Burnside and young Khan,' Jacob's arms opened in their traditional gesture of welcome. 'I heard your footsteps. I am glad you did not sleep too soundly to hear Sengila. The birds – they are coming.'

Against the dark navy of the night sky, a huddle of black specs surged towards them.

'*Jacob, do something,*' Jack gasped. Then he remembered. 'Sorry, I forgot,' he mumbled, rubbing his eyes to get the sleep out of them. *Gosh, he did feel tired.* 'You sure it's the birds.'

'Sengila brought me the news when he saw them gathering in the mountains. But why has it taken so long – it is way past midnight.'

'Perhaps he had a change of heart,' suggested Jack half-joking.

'Mendorun has no heart and no pity either.'

As Jacob spoke, the moon disappeared behind a cloud – a cloud which began to change shape, growing legs and horns.

A single bird headed the long V-formation, their huge wings moving steadily to the accompaniment of a soft-drumming sound, Taa te-te-te-te taa – Taa te-te-te-te taa – Taa te-te-te-te taa, like someone gently brushing the surface of a snare drum. It grew louder and faster, becoming recognisable as the sound of giant wings beating the air. And yet, if the watching party had not expected the black menace, the column would have slipped by unnoticed as yet another flock of migrating birds; except for one vital difference – each bird carried something in its beak.

'Jacob, is that the poison?'

The birds drew nearer. If Jack had possessed a ruler, long enough to draw a vertical line from the sky down to the ground, it would have landed at the farthest edge of the fields that kept the kingdom supplied with fruits and vegetables.

Jack clenched his fists, muttering under his breath, *please don't let them succeed. Let Jacob be right.*

Then the wildebeest struck.

It was like that occasion at school, when his class had watched a black and white movie about the Battle for Britain, which took place at the beginning of the Second World War. First, there were the enemy in their Messerschmitt, the planes weaving and ducking, calling warnings to one another on their intercom. Then the Spitfires arrived, diving down out of the sun their guns blazing, until the enemy fell to earth in an inferno of burning metal. Except the Messerschmitt weren't aircraft, they were black-bodied crows, lurching and flailing helplessly around in the night sky as the wildebeest launched attack after attack. Their hooves struck sparks off the fuselage of the enemy, with the ferocity and speed of the blows. Their horns resounded with a sharp crack, as they charged head first into the body of the now powerless birds. The birds fought back using their beaks, their claws, and their flying skills as weapons. But, as in real battle, the Messerschmitt hadn't a hope against the speed and savagery of the Spitfire, so the hapless crows stood no chance against the demonic-madness of the wildebeest. Wings torn and bleeding, breasts gutted with entrails hanging out, the black birds were overcome, their bodies plummeting silently to earth.

Jack counted twenty bodies lying lifeless, a crumpled mass of black feathers. Not one survivor and only two of the wildebeest lost, as casualties of war. There was a deathly silence – the battle was over.

Jacob stirred. 'Now, I will go to bed. I will wake you both early for there is still much to be done. Goodnight.'

The boys stared after the disappearing silhouette, the lion at his side, and then at each other – speechless.

'Nuffin' to say is there,' Khan said at last.

Jack shook his head, words failing him. 'I think we'd better go back to bed,' he managed.

Chapter Eighteen

The Blue Light

Jack slept, a long, long, deep sleep, sloughing off the nightmares of the previous days. He woke reluctantly to a hammering on his door.

It opened and Khan entered, followed by a servant carrying a tray of food.

'You OK. I just woke up, too,' said his friend, his face erupting into its lopsided grin.

The servant crossed to the window and, pulling wide the shutters, placed the heavy tray down on a little table by the window. Jack leapt out of bed. Running out onto the balcony, he took a deep breath to fill his lungs. It had rained in the night and the fields looked fresh and green, the little irrigation channels full of water. In the distance, vast mountain peaks basked in the early-morning light; the small valley, little known to the outside world, chosen by Prince Salah as a place of safety for his people.

And scum-bags like Saladin and Mendorun shouldn't be allowed to destroy it, Jack told himself. His stomach rumbled noisily. 'I hope there's plenty to eat, I'm starving.'

There was; hot bread with rice and vegetables, yoghurt and honey cakes, with coconut milk to drink.

'That Jacob's a rum bloke, but not bad,' Khan said, munching noisily. ''E gave me some stuff for me cuts.' He held out his arms. The last time Jack had seen them, they'd been covered in bandages and, before that, blood; falling in large beads on the ground where the talons of the crow had ripped into his flesh. Now, they were nearly healed, only narrow white lines left to show where the skin had knitted together.

'I can see why ye wanted to stop that Mendorun bloke messin' up this place,' he said, gazing out over the ramparts towards the football ground. 'It's nice. *Jack?*'

'Mmm.'

'What 'appens now?'

Jack yawned. 'I guess Jacob will take you home. I've got to get back too.' He sat up suddenly wide awake. 'Jeez! *And by this afternoon.*' He lapsed back in his chair, once again reworking his itinerary. If Bud didn't recover soon … Jacob would have to ferry him to Rabat using the jewelled box. It didn't much matter how he got to the hotel, as long as he got there before Barney called the police.

'Ye know them prayer-mutterers. Can 'e really do anyfin' for 'em?'

'To be honest, I had no idea Jacob was this powerful.' Jack ladled another helping of vegetables and rice on to his plate. 'Do you have to go? You could stay here. Saleem would like you to – and Jacob.'

'Ye're goin'.' Khan's frowned, his eyebrows a straight furrow.

'But I've got a home. You haven't, except the streets.'

'I got me mates.'

'But you could have a proper home here and go to school,' Jack said, his voice rising impatiently.

'School! Ye're jokin'.'

Jack pulled a face. 'It's better than scavenging for a living.'

A knock sounded at the door, a face peeping round it.

Jack jumped to his feet, beaming. '*Yazim*! I heard you were safe.'

The boy gave a half bow. 'Have you come here to play football with us, Sir Jack?' He mimed kicking a ball with his bare feet.

Jack laughed. 'Great footballer,' he explained to Khan. 'Not this time, Yazim. I'm not staying long. Perhaps, when I visit next.'

'That will be good. I am especially good at scoring goals,' the boy boasted, smiling shyly at Khan. 'I have a message from the master. He says you are to go with him. He has camels waiting.'

The two boys tore down the stairs, laughing and joking, and out into the bright new day; the sun sparkling on the roof tiles, as if trying to apologise for all the horrid things Mendorun had thrown at them.

They emerged into sunlight on the far side of the postern. Jacob was already there, the waiting camels chewing the cud and gazing superciliously at the world around them. The sorcerer brushed his fingers through the air in greeting, directing the animals to their knees so Khan and Jack could scramble on.

'Want to race?' Jack called.

Khan's lopsided grin flashed briefly. His camel, responding to the click of the reins, set off in a lumbering run with Jack's immediately behind him.

Side by side, the two animals hurtled over the open plain towards the nearby hills, their saddles and riders bouncing violently in the air with their uneven gait. Khan grinned triumphantly as Jack's beast, hissing with displeasure, was beaten into second place.

'Beat'ye,' he shouted thumping his camel violently on its rump in gratitude.

'You've done this before,' Jack accused, put out that he'd lost.

'*You bet!*' Khan slid to the ground. 'One of me jobs was to feed and water them camels on market day, so I 'as a ride when the boss isn't lookin'.'

'You never said,' Jack's tone was indignant.

'Ye never asked.'

'Asked what?' enquired Jacob, catching up with them.

'If I could ride a camel,' replied Khan, grinning.

'I hear from Jack you can also open doors?'

'Yeah, I can; but before ye ask, sir, I don't know 'ow.'

Jacob dismounted, his robes fluttering slightly in the light air. 'Follow me closely. Last time, I forgot to warn Jack the cave was invisible.'

'*Invisible?*' muttered Khan. 'Fer real?'

Jacob smiled at the boy walking beside him, leaving Jack to bring up the rear. '*Can you do other things?*'

'Sometimes I can see fings,' Khan admitted grudgingly, as if uncertain whether to trust him or not.

'Can you see the cave?'

Jacob stopped abruptly, standing back to let the boy pass by him, their four-legged transport volubly protesting the change in plan and spitting noisily. Khan hesitated. A moment later the space where he'd been standing was empty.

'How did you know?' gasped Jack amazed.

'I can feel his aura. It is very, very small but it is there.'

'Are you going to tell him?'

Jacob shook his head. 'Go first, my Lord Burnside, otherwise you will get lost again.'

Jack grinned cheerfully, his camel obligingly following him through the invisible air around the mouth of the cave.

It remained dusk in the cave, a shimmering blue shadow lifting the gloom. Khan stood transfixed, gawking at the space around him hardly able to believe his eyes.

'We had better tether the beasts,' said Jacob, ignoring the surprised boy, simply blowing the embers of the fire into life again.

Jack hurriedly retrieved the camel's harness from Khan's nerveless fingers, tethering both animals in their accustomed place, their cumbersome bodies blocking all sight of the inner sanctum.

Khan joined the other two at the fire, staring at Jacob in awe.

'You remind me of me, when I first met Jacob,' said Jack, remembering how overwhelming he had found everything.

'It's …'

'Weird! Come on, Khan, you've met some pretty odd things over the past couple of days, surely you can take an invisible cave in your stride.'

'Yeah, I can,' the boy retorted. 'But not one *I can see*. Why can I do that?' he asked the sorcerer, who was ferreting about in one of the saddlebags.

'It happens,' said Jacob, his tone as casual as if Khan had confessed to being ambidextrous. 'I will make tea,' he changed the subject.

'Jacob, what's happened to the boys?' said Jack, secretly thrilled at Khan's obvious confusion, which was only fair after the boy had beaten him in the camel race.

'They have already been escorted home, my Lord Burnside.'

'At least you could have let us say goodbye,' he protested.

Jacob shook his head. 'For what purpose?' He leant forward balancing the water pot on the glowing embers. A hiss of steam erupted from the fire. 'They would not have remembered you.'

'Why?' said Khan, instantly suspicious.

'The images they carried with them were so vivid, they could not have recovered. I have simply removed all memory from the time they were captured. All they will recollect is becoming lost in the desert. It was kinder, although I expect them to get into trouble for both had anxious parents waiting for news. I explained they had been found wandering without water and no further questions were asked; both families relieved they were safe, after the disappearance of so many children.'

'Tell me about it. We kept off the streets at night, 'cos'a the carts,' said Khan eager to make up for his suspicions. 'When did they go?'

'Early – before daybreak – with Saleem. Did you lose many children from Pulah, young Khan?'

'Some.' Khan shuffled about, the rock hard and uneven with

sharp edges, despite having a carpet laid on top of it. 'It were real scary. But what's 'appened to the other kids they took?'

Jacob indicated the blue light. 'That is what we are hoping to hear.' He rose to his feet. 'Let us discover if this pestilential animal is once again alive.'

The blue light disappeared, leaving only the glow from the fire. Shadows leapt from crack to crack in the roughly hewn walls, as the boys moved an arm to drink their tea or stretched a leg to ease muscles cramped from sitting on the hard ground. Jacob reappeared with the wooden statue. He placed it on the ground to reflect the firelight, creating a neat shadow on the wall behind.

Jack bit his lip, anxiously waiting. For a moment nothing happened, the silence broken only by the chomping of the camels at the hay bag and the hissing of the fire. A flame shot high into the air. As it did, the shadow of the camel stretched and yawned, growing and growing. It continued to swell, until it overflowed onto the roof. There came a noise of someone spitting, '*Pfliipft!*' and the leering shadow turned and looked straight at them.

'*Bud!*' shouted Jack, over-riding Jacob's muttered, 'The Gods *be prais-ed,*' and Khan's loud exclamation, '*Blimey!*'

'Salaam Aleikum,' the doleful voice greeted them. 'It is good to discover I am not forgotten.'

'*Bud! It's great!*' Jack leapt to his feet and patted the soft nose projecting from the wall. 'I told you he came alive.'

'Only just, and even now I doubt it,' said the mournful voice.

'I don't think I'll dare doubt anyfin' again,' said Khan. 'I called Jack a liar but 'e was telling the truuf all along.'

'You were not to blame, young Khan.'

'*Khan! Master! What manner of boy is this?*'

'*Hsst, beast!*'

The commanding tones of Jacob's voice stopped everyone in

their tracks. He leapt to his feet, his eyes locked with those of the camel. The atmosphere changed becoming fraught with tension. Jack held his breath, staring anxiously from one to the other. Angry exchanges were part and parcel of the on-going warfare between Bud and the sorcerer. But what made this different, neither had erupted into the usual stream of wild insults. Instead, they stayed frighteningly silent.

'Khan is from Pulah,' Jacob broke the deafening silence. 'He is a friend of Lord Burnside – that is all.'

Bud turned his head away and spat noisily. '*Pfliipft!* Why are we talking in my language, master? There is something here I do not understand, for the little infidel has no knowledge of Arabic.'

The atmosphere began to relax.

'He does now, Bud,' Jack said proudly, wondering what had caused the clash. 'That was down to Jacob. Thank heavens he did. If you remember, you weren't about.'

'Beast? I need you to tell me what happened?'

Bud glared, his top lip pulled back to expose his teeth stained yellow from eating hay made from corn stalks. 'I will tell you but only because there is little time to lose. Otherwise, I would remain silent for a day or two in order to annoy you. However, while I talk I would like to be seen receiving sustenance, like those four-legged dromedaries, who doubtless are treated to the finest of hay made from dates – while I, the most loyal of beasts, is forced to eat chaff.'

Jack ran over to the wall, where some small bales of hay were stacked. Grabbing one, he propped it against the wall. Much to Khan's astonishment, the animal stretched further into the room, tearing hungrily at the wispy stalks.

'As you asked, oh master, I entered the fortress and scoured the passageways. It was there I found the children.'

'Are they OK?' said Khan, breaking his astonished silence.

Bud hissed, staring down his nose at the boy. 'May I to lower myself to speak with the street boy?' he said haughtily. 'Or do you prohibit that as well?'

'Bud, stop being a wus,' Jack stroked the soft pink nose. 'I know you hate strangers but Khan's my friend. He saved my life.'

'Then, young street boy, if necessary I will save your life, after that of the young master.'

Jack grinned. 'So why have the soldiers been going round the countryside stealing children?'

'I will not speak of that,' Bud said, breaking into the hidden language he shared only with Jacob.

'Why not?' said Jack, aware Khan felt as impatient as him. He watched Jacob's hands slow down and become still. 'It can't be any worse than what we've already been through,' he added, suddenly feeling scared again.

'It is worse, my Lord Burnside,' Jacob replied gravely. 'How were you captured, oh curs-ed one?'

The shadow on the wall presented both an intriguing and mesmerising sight. For the most part it remained a shadowy figure, with only its nose and part of its head three dimensional. Lifting its long neck free of the wall, it turned its head grinding its teeth against the rock face, as if it had developed an itch on its back.

Khan's expression became almost comical in its bewilderment, unable to grasp how an animal with a stone stomach found it possible to eat, never mind scratch.

'Even I cannot prevail if I am trapped by light,' Bud glanced balefully at the three humans.

'Which light?' said Jack, wondering if the camel had ranged as far as the room with the birds.

'I do not know which light, infidel. All lights are the same, as *all boys* are the same, particularly if *they are street boys,*' the camel snapped, put out by all the questioning. 'I instantly became a wooden statue, the only power left to me – to contact you, my Lord Burnside.'

'You did, Bud, and I've got bruises on my back to prove it.'

'It is mystifying why christians are such weak race,' the camel retorted, becoming fractionally less grouchy as he recovered from his ordeal.

Jack laughed.

'It was Saladin – *may he be curs-ed for what he did to Prince Salah* – who recognised the shape and told Mendorun. He knew at once that I possessed great magic and squeezed me tightly, as if he could force out all my secrets. Fortunately for me he did not,' he added contemptuously. 'That is all. I trust I am exempt from any more probing about the light,' Bud finished haughtily. 'Master, will you tell me the infidel's story?'

'Much has happened, beast,' Jacob said, telling the story of the capture from the camp at Asfah – including Betsy's part in it, which made Bud snort with indignation – and lastly the threat to the people of the kingdom, the poison carried by the giant birds. 'Mendorun will have realised by now they are not returning,' he ended his tale 'He will not accept that.'

The camel gazed mournfully first at Jacob then at Jack, shaking his head all the time – as if ridding himself of a troublesome fly. 'Have you set a watch, master?'

'Sengila is in the mountains overlooking the fortress.' Jacob raised his shoulders, his hands lifted in their traditional gesture, palms uppermost, fingers splayed, absolving himself of any responsibility for future events.

There was silence.

'Sir, Jack and me, we still want to hear about them kids?'

Jacob hands flew into the air as if to object. Placing them silently back on his lap, he said quietly, 'Mendorun has changed the captured children into birds.'

'*That's impossible!*' Jack's voice collided with Khan's, '*Ye're makin' it up.*'

'Street boy, I do not fabricate stories,' Bud replied offended.

It was all Jack could do not to burst out laughing, despite the fearful news, since the camel spent most of its time disguising the truth.

'We still have to rescue them.'

'To what end, my Lord Burnside,' Jacob said. 'From what the beast has told me, they are beyond my help. All that is left is to destroy the fortress.'

'*Ye can't do that,*' Khan burst out. 'You 'elped Abu and Shahi, you can 'elp these kids.'

'Those two boys were traumatised only, young Khan. They still had minds. I have no magic to restore lost minds.'

'THEN YOU FIND SOME, JACOB,' Jack yelled, losing his temper. "*Cos I'm going to get them out of that place if it's the last thing I do.*'

'And I'll come wiv ye,' Khan added.

Jacob tore at his hair. 'Why did I ever burden myself with this irrational being of a boy. Why cannot you accept what I say?'

'*Because I can't,* I *have to rescue them,*' Jack thundered. 'You can't! You'd ring every alarm bell in sight, if you tried. Anyway, I owe it to Yazim,' he said more quietly. 'He's fine but it could easily have been him.'

'But, my Lord Burnside,' pleaded Jacob, 'how do I prevent danger once again overcoming you? I failed before. I cannot let you go through it again.'

Anger flew into the air, the atmosphere once again fraught with tension. Jack, his fists clenched tight, his face set stubbornly; Jacob, aware of the greater picture, distraught that his warnings were being ignored.

It was the camel that broke the silence.

'Master, in a foolish moment long ago, I promised the infidel I would help him rescue his friend. If I am to redeem my word, I will accompany him on this foolhardy errand. I will keep him safe.'

Bud's tone was his usual gloomy one, but the large brown eyes were serious and his mouth held not a trace of a sneer.

'If I wait long enough, I expect the entire universe will offer their help to make up a rescue party.' Jacob screeched. 'You, beast, did not see the two young boys I sent back to their homes. *Such evil, such wickedness has to be destroyed,*' he roared. 'I must act before Mendorun does, for I am sure – as the sun will set – that Mendorun will strike *and strike us hard.* It makes no sense to put the rest in danger in order to rescue beings that are beyond help.'

He leapt to his feet, gripping the air with his hands, as if he wanted to pull the rock ceiling down on top of them. Bud gazed intently at his master, the silence broken only by the camels moving restlessly at the back of the cave.

'I beg you to think again,' he said, more calmly now. He bent low over the fire making fresh tea, simply to keep his hands employed, handing out honey sweetmeats for the two boys to eat with the hot beverage. 'For such a rescue will demand time. Time we do not have. There is a silence in the air which worries me. I fear for our safety.'

Furiously angry with himself, Jack buried his face in his glass, wishing his words back. Once again he had burst out in childish rage, not bothering about the consequences. Jacob was right. Even now Mendorun was probably dreaming up some terrible revenge. The only thing Jacob could do was destroy the fortress and everything in it, before the sorcerer had time to put his plans into action. But he couldn't because he, Jack, was hell-bent on rescuing some nameless children that thought they were birds.

Even worse; Jack drew in a painful breath. *He could kiss his football career goodbye.* He might have got away with it till evening. Even then, Andy and Rob would have stacked up that many lies he'd be paying off his debt for ever. But any later than that … Angry tears brushed against his eyelids.

'Sir Jacob?' It was Khan. 'Prince Saleem said them soldiers used tunnels to break into the palace. Could we do that?'

Jack held his breath. When Saladin had overrun the palace, he'd done so by digging through the mountains, his army emerging from the cellars. But after the rescue, the tunnels had been blocked.

Jacob didn't reply, staring pensively at the fire, one hand stroking his beard. Bud stopped chewing, eyeing the sorcerer with interest.

'It is possible,' Jacob said reluctantly. 'But Lord Burnside, I beg you to think before you embark on this foolhardy mission; I may not succeed in helping the children. Are you prepared for that?'

Football against the lives of kids – no contest. 'But you'll help them, Jacob, I know you will,' Jack said, forcing himself to sound optimistic.

The sorcerer sighed heavily, sensing defeat. He rose to his feet and vanishing into the grotto, reappeared a moment later with two wooden carvings. 'They may be of use.' He handed them to Jack. 'I will give you till sunset. Then I go to destroy the fortress.'

Chapter Nineteen

The Tunnels

Carrying a lantern, Jack and Khan followed Jacob along a maze of corridors, mostly used by servants when the heavy winter rains made the gardens impassable. Well lit and wide, with neatly tiled floors, a steep flight of steps led down into a dusty passageway. Lined with cellars, these were crammed full of barrels and boxes covered in cobwebs. Eventually, their way was blocked by a vast iron gate. Pulling a key from the bunch at his waist, Jacob opened it. The passageway drifted on for a few metres before ending abruptly, sealed off by a wall of stone.

'Is that the entrance to the tunnels?' Jack said, staring nervously at the wall.

Jacob gave a curt nod, withdrawing the jewelled box from his sleeve. A blinding flash of light leapt from the open lid and a visible charge of electricity, a thousand times more powerful than Khan had used to open the locks, flew across the gap. The wall rumbled and shook violently, as if some ferocious beast was trying to break through. A crack zigzagged down to the ground, the stone on either side crumpling into dust.

Jacob sighed and, for a moment, appeared very troubled. 'Remember, I will stay my hand only till sunset.'

'Don't worry, Jacob, we'll be back. Come on, Khan, let's get going.'

'Not without me, you're not.' Saleem appeared, his ready smile flashing warmly. 'I heard about the kids, so I'm coming.'

'My Lord Prince! *No!* You cannot! If you insist, I must send for guards to make sure you are safe.'

'No need, Pops, I'll look after him.'

Mercedes, wearing a black tunic over trousers and long boots, a deep-maroon scarf obscuring the lower half of her face, strolled up out of the darkness of the corridor, not a hair out of place.

Khan stared at the girl, speechless with astonishment.

'*My daughter – no, no, no!*' Jacob's hands tore round and round, like sprinters on a track.

'Sorry, Pops. I'm goin'. Anyway they need me. You look after the palace and I'll look after them.'

'Look after us! *Blimey, you've got a cheek.* Ye're a girl!'

'Khan, this is not just any-old girl,' laughed Saleem. 'I promise you, Mercedes is a great warrior.'

Jacob's shoulders shot up into the air descending slowly. 'My daughter, if I let you go, it is Jack Burnside who is in charge.'

'Gee, Pops, *that's not fair. Why can't I lead*, I fight better than him any day.'

'Because Jack Burnside has been up against Mendorun before, and you haven't, my rose of the Nile. You can go only if you agree to that condition.'

'OK, Pops,' Mercedes glared belligerently, her voice sulky. '*But it's not fair*. I hate being a girl,' she grumbled. 'I'm never allowed to do anything.'

'Khan, you'd better light the lamp,' Jack said.

Khan immediately set a match to the wick. It flared, illuminating the darkness of the tunnel ahead. Jack placed the two wooden camels close to the wall, allowing the sneering face of Bud to come alive, followed by a surprised-looking Betsy.

'Keep them safe, beast. If there is a choice between the safety of my children and that of the prisoners in the fortress, there is no choice.' Bud bowed his head. 'And remember you have less than six hours till sunset.'

'Mercedes, you ride with me,' Jack instructed. 'Khan, tie the lamp to Betsy's saddle. He can see in the dark; we can't.'

Removing the wooden carvings from his jacket pocket, Jack ran his thumb over their smooth surface, admiring the skill needed to produce birds that looked both fierce and proud, their eyes and beaks menacing in the half-light. He stowed them in one of the saddle bags, thinking eagles a strange choice when they were travelling underground. If only Jacob would trust him enough to share his thoughts as to what he believed might or might not happen.

Their harness ringing, the camels set off down the long passageway, the silhouette of the sorcerer fading gradually into the darkness. A shiver of excitement ran down Jack's spine. Once again, he and Bud, his most extraordinary friend, were headed into adventure. And if he hadn't been feeling so miserable about losing his place in the football team, he would have been both excited *and* happy.

The passageway ran straight – a long tube cut under the same fields that Khan and Jack had raced only that morning. A single rail track flowed down its centre; clear evidence as to how the invading army had stolen up on the palace, so quickly and quietly. But the sound of drilling? Jack stared nervously at the roof, wondering how they had managed to cut through rock without being heard, bothered by the idea of tons of rock and earth crashing down on them.

Bud, with Betsy following, jogged along quite comfortably; Khan and Saleem chatting away like old friends. Jack didn't join in, still worried that his reckless action might result in serious repercussions for the kingdom. He gazed down at his watch, surprised to find the hours speeding past – just when he needed them to slow down. In front of them the tunnel, high-lighted by the lamps on the camels' harness, unrolled into the darkness without any end in sight. Alarmed, Jack remembered how long it had taken for Betsy to travel even half-way across the mountains. There was no way they could be back by sunset, unless he went on alone – with Bud.

Khan's voice broke into his thoughts. 'Jack, there's a light.'

'Mercedes, you and Saleem wait here,' Jack called, praying they had reached their destination. Anxiously, he checked the time again.

The tunnel opened into a wide cavern which resembled the goods-yard of a railway station, littered with flatbed trucks. Tunnels radiated out of it, like spokes in a wheel, a series of railway lines emerging in the cave.

Khan leapt up on one of the trucks. 'What'a these, Jack?'

'Trucks,' Jack said dejectedly, dismayed to find they were still a long way from their destination. He noticed Khan's puzzled expression, 'Have you never seen a railway before?'

'No, we only 'ave camels where I live. But them trucks carried men. An' they stopped 'ere.' Khan showed Jack a mass of dusty footprints on the dry earth.

The two boys slipped back into the darkness where Saleem and Mercedes waited.

'Safe?' said Saleem.

'Yes, but there's a problem. Bud and Betsy can't go any further. The tunnels are all lit from here. They'll have to go back.'

'I cannot leave you, young master, I am not permitted.' Bud's harness rang, the sound of the bells echoing against the rock wall.

'Stuff that,' said Jack. 'You're no use as a wooden statue. Anyhow, Jacob needs you – he didn't want you to come with us in the first place.'

'Is that a guess, infidel, or do you have evidence as to my acccursed master's state of mind?' sneered the camel.

Jack grinned. 'Evidence, Bud. Jacob's hands broke the world's speed record, and that only happens when something's really bothering him. So we're going on.' Jack patted the camel's broad back. 'We haven't any choice.'

'Then we will wait, infidel. But hurry.'

No one spoke although Jack knew Saleem felt as anxious as him, his merry smile flashing on and off like a traffic beacon. Still, being afraid had never stopped Saleem in the past. But Khan and Mercedes? They were as much bothered as if they were planning an outing in the countryside. Did either of them have a clue what it felt like to be really terrified – so scared that your knees knocked together and you felt sick. Even trapped in the cave by the lion, hadn't frightened Khan for long.

Quickly removing Bud's saddlebags, Jack slipped them over his shoulder. Saleem had already stripped Betsy and was carrying the lantern and a coil of rope. They headed into the cavern and Saleem ran over to inspect the trucks.

'There's no time for that,' Jack called impatiently. 'Come on.'

''Ang on a mo, Jack, Saleem's up to somefin'.'

'You're dead-right,' laughed Mercedes. 'When Saleem wasn't playin' football with you, Jack, he was at the station watchin' trains.'

'What's a train?'

'Like a lot of cars stuck together, Khan. They run on tracks like this one.' The young Prince crawled out from under the truck. 'When this is over, we'll go to England,' he promised. 'They have the real thing there – steam trains. Look, if we can work that lever...' He nodded towards a row of levers positioned by the side of the track. 'We can use that truck to take us through the tunnel.'

'But why to go to all that trouble?' said Jack sounding puzzled.

'For the kids,' crowed Mercedes. 'Genius, Saleem.'

Saleem ran over to a truck resting on its side across the rails. 'But we've got to move this thing first.'

Putting their shoulders to the heavy wooden platform, they heaved it slowly upright, their muscles straining. It shuddered as if unsure which way to fall. Then, with a loud thud and a flurry of dust, it toppled heavily away from the tracks. Wave after wave of sound echoed round the chamber, like the aftermath of an explosion. Gradually the echoes died away, silence taking over once more.

'If they didn't hear that little lot, we've got a long way to go,' Jack called.

Together, the three boys tugged at the lever. Stiff from disuse, it moved grudgingly and, with loud protestations, the rail inched into its new position, heading into the right-hand tunnel.

Using the wheel as a step, Jack climbed onto the flatbed, immediately jumping down again.

'Hang on a mo, I forgot something.' He ran back to the tunnel, where the two camels waited, scooping handfuls of pebbles and small rocks into a mound. 'Just making sure we can get back,' he said cheerfully, giving Mercedes a hand up. 'I'd hate to get lost down here.

In the middle of the flatbed, a metal dome was set into the wood and, beneath the platform a series of pistons connected lengths of iron rod to the wheels. Saleem climbed up brandishing a lever. Inserting it into a metal socket at the base of the dome, he pushed down hard. The flatbed lurched violently. Overbalancing, Jack grabbed Mercedes to stop her falling off.

'Sorry, wrong way,' said Saleem cheerfully. He moved to the other side of the metal dome, using the socket on that side. 'Give me a hand, Khan.'

Somewhat reluctantly, the flatbed truck began to roll towards the tunnel entrance, quickly picking up speed, the only sound a faint clicking as they swept over the intersection between the rail ends.

The minutes ticked past. Each time they rounded a bend Jack expected it to be the last, anxiously watching the time.

'Stop worrying.' Puffed from working the lever, Saleem stood back to catch his breath, letting Khan to take a turn. 'We'll make it.'

As he spoke the truck rounded yet another corner, a gate barring their way. It rolled to a stop, its nose pressed up against a wide span of iron work. On the far side, the passage broadened to accommodate a huge wheel with stout lengths of cable wrapped around it. They had arrived.

'Now what?' Mercedes asked the question first.

'Can you open it, Khan?'

'I'll 'ave a go.' Leaping down from the truck, he studied the gate intently.

'Pull the other one,' Mercedes scoffed.

'He may not be much good at anything else,' Jack grinned at her, 'but he's wicked at opening locks.'

'Sorry, Khan, no one told me.'

Khan swung round, half of his face lighting up. 'It's not somefin' you tell people.'

As if pressing them against a wall, Khan directed his hands towards the wheel. Nothing happened, nothing breaking the silence except the sound of his breathing.

'Ye'll 'ave to be ready,' he said. 'I ain't strong enuff to 'old it up.'

'How will we get back?' Saleem jumped down. He crouched next to the spikes; his stance like that of a sprinter on a race track waiting for the starter's whistle.

'There's a handle,' Jack pointed to the wheel, a large turning handle resting in the six o'clock position. 'Getting back's easy, don't worry.'

Khan opened his fingers stretching them wide. A living current of electricity sprang from his fingertips and leapt through the air towards the wheel. A loud grating noise filled the mineshaft and the wheel moved stiffly, the links of the chain tightening. The gate jerked upwards, wrapping a length of chain around the wheel, and again and again, until it was high enough for a body to pass through.

Khan stepped forwards, his nose pressed against the iron bars. He raised his hands. Once more, the gate jerked upwards.

'NOW!' Jack shouted ducking underneath, Saleem and Mercedes quickly following. The gate hesitated in the air as Khan dived through headfirst, before tumbling noisily into the ground again, its pointed tips digging into the ground.

'Everyone OK?'

'Fine.' Picking themselves up, Mercedes and Saleem brushed the dust off their clothes.

Khan remained on the ground. Unmoving, his face was parchment white, his entire body shaking as if he had the ague. Jack slid to the ground beside him and put his arm around the trembling boy.

'I feel terrible. *What's 'appened, Jack*? I ain't got any strengf left. I can't move.'

'Not sure. I think Jacob would say you'd used up all your magnetic force. You need an energy boost.'

'Jack?' Khan let his head drop forward with exhaustion. 'Am I a sorcerer like Jacob?'

'You're not like Jacob, but I think so. Is there any water?'

Saleem tore open the saddlebag, pulling out a bottle of water and some of the honey cakes, left from their previous journey on Betsy.

Khan sipped at the water gratefully, munching at one of the square of pastry, hard and gluey after nearly two days in the saddlebag. Gradually, the colour crept back into his face, the sugar surging through his body to replenish his lost energy.

'I tell you what though, Khan,' Mercedes said, her tone amiable. 'You're a pretty-peculiar street boy.'

'I don't wan'ter be,' glowered Khan pushing himself away from the gate. 'I wan'ter be me. I don't like all this weird stuff.'

'Well, if you've got it, Khan – *flaunt it* – that's what I say.'

'Girls! What do they know!' he retorted contemptuously, rising slowly to his feet.

'Can you go on?'

'Yeah, Jack, but I wish I were back in Pulah.'

'Me, too. So let's find the kids and go home.'

Chapter Twenty

The Bird-Children

The passage widened, plunging them into a cesspit of the most foul, sick-making smell. Holding their noses, they rounded the corner. A great swell of noise hit them – the sound of birds chattering. The walls of the huge cavern were smeared with bird droppings and in the centre of the room, taking up a vast amount of space, was a cage of steel. The smell came from the cage.

How cruel was Jack's first reaction, watching the black and brown bodies smash their wings against its steel uprights. And it wasn't only crows beating their wings helplessly in the overcrowded space. It was as if a vast net had been cast into the sky, trapping everything that moved; sparrows, blackbirds, crows and linnets, canaries and swifts. Even swallows caught in their migratory flight, unable to use their flying expertise, were among the birds in the cage.

His eyes flew down into the dark confusion of the cage floor. With a sickening jolt, he saw it was covered with small boys, their arms flapping in imitation of a bird, pecking helplessly at the food scattered on the cage floor.

'Come on,' Mercedes said. 'I wonder what else that megalomaniac's bin up to.'

In one corner, a pile of dead birds added to the stench. Ignoring it, she moved on to inspect the smaller cage in the far corner, her face quite expressionless.

Like the first, this held more evidence of Mendorun's evil ambitions. Children lifted from the streets of Asfah or Pulah, where they had been innocently playing one moment and the next had vanished; stolen away and kept like mad dogs in a cage. These, at least, were sitting quietly on the ground like humans, not hopping round a cage.

Suddenly, one of the children moved. 'Prince Saleem,' he shouted and leapt to his feet. Two others jumped up beside him; the rest remaining silent and unmoving.

'Sir Prince! *I knew you would come.*' The three children rushed to the bars, pounding on them in a desperate effort to be free.

'What's happened here?' asked Saleem,

'They've bin 'ypnotised,' said Khan.

'We was very lucky, Sir Prince,' the boy said. 'We all tried very hard to stop it. But they wore us down. There's only three of us left now.' He indicated the girl and boy. 'Mina and Abdul. I am called Hamid. Please, sir, get us out?'

Leaving the three boys, Mercedes wandered across the room and peeped through a small pane of glass, set in the top of a door. Reassured they were undetected, she pulled it open.

Sunlight surged in. Jack followed Mercedes out into the fresh air, the stench of the cage making his stomach heave. They found themselves in a lava bubble, its roof open to the sky, where the black basalt had solidified into a convex shape. Here, half-a-dozen cages had been erected under the open space, each one containing a small child. Cross-legged and motionless, they sat staring at nothing. Tethered to the top of the cage, and bathed in golden light, perched a monstrous crow. The child in its cage was immersed in blue. No wires or plugs and sockets, the light simply existed, independent of anything; offering yet another clue as to how powerful Mendorun had become. Jack bent down, noticing a stream of green bubbles flowing upwards from the child.

'Saleem, come and look at this?' he called, poking his head round the door.

Turning pale, Saleem gazed speechless at the dozing giants, the first he had seen. Even Jack had to admit, these were awesome.

'So they weren't all destroyed,' Saleem said bitterly, finally breaking the silence.

'What's 'e doin' with this lot?' whispered Khan, joining them. Behind him, Hamid watched nervously from the doorway.

'He wants to create a familiar,' Jack explained, remembering Jacob's story.

'What's that?'

'Something like Bud – a bird with brains, if you like.'

'An' why the kids?'

'He's using their minds, their energy, their spirit – whatever you want to call it – so the crows can think and act independently. That blue light is a negative source, which makes the child weak. The gold light is the positive. It feeds the crow and turns it into a monstrous carbuncle. I s'pose the green is the energy seeping from the child. At least, I think so.'

'And the boys back there?' said Mercedes.

'I guess they're the ones he's already used,' Jack said miserably. 'Hang on a mo.'

When the volcano had erupted gas had become trapped underground, sculpting out a narrow tunnel. Jack ran along it, his trainers making no sound on the rock floor. He eased open the door at the far end. As he suspected, it led into the room of golden light. The room appeared as he'd left it, except there was no golden light and no birds. *At least Jacob had destroyed most of them.* Closing the door, he slipped back to the lava bubble.

'Come on. Let's round up the kids.'

Mercedes pulled open the door of the cage. 'They're not locked.' She hesitated, her hand stalled in the air.

'Don't worry about the blue stuff, it won't hurt you – at least, not unless you're trapped in it.' Jack grabbed the hand of the traumatised youngster and hauled him to his feet. 'Mendorun's just about cracked it; these kids are just empty shells.'

Saleem was already heading out of the room, a child in each hand, Khan holding the heavy door open with his foot. They followed docilely, their faces blank.

Mercedes walked her charge to the door. 'Let's get them to Pops, Jack. If anyone can fix them, he can.'

Jack sighed, envying Mercedes her optimism. He gasped aloud as the door closed on the fresh air, the fetid stench enveloping him like a blanket.

'Hamid, you and your friends follow Mercedes. We'll bring the rest.'

Taking the six docile forms with her, the girl ushered them across the floor, vanishing into the shelter of the tunnel. Hamid, Mina and Abdul followed, herding a little group of children all totally unaware they had been rescued.

Now, only the cage of birds was left. Jack hesitated, steeling himself to face it. He tried to count the children, reaching twelve. But it was impossible to be accurate, the hopping shapes continually disappearing among the flocks of birds. Whatever the number, at least thirty children had been stolen, possibly more, if some had died. The thought made him feel sick.

Ignoring the filth, Khan opened the cage and went in, his feet slipping in his borrowed sandals. He made a grab for one of the bird-children. It squawked loudly and tried to bite him, its arms flapping wildly. In an instant the cage was a whirling mass; the children perched on the ground as panicky as the wild creatures in the air, flinging themselves at the bars with frustration at not being able to fly.

'Saleem?' called Khan. 'Can you 'elp us, this lot's a bit tricky.'

Working together, they cornered one of the children. Khan held it by the shoulders with Saleem and Jack taking a leg each. It thrashed wildly, squawking indignantly. They staggered over the slimy mess towards the cage door, struggling to grip the slippery body seesawing up and down.

'This is hopeless,' groaned Saleem as the child escaped and, with a flutter of arms, fled back into the cage. 'We'll have to leave these.'

'We're takin' 'em,' Khan, his face set in a mutinous frown. 'I recognise them.' He pointed at two figures pecking the grain near his feet. 'They're from Pulah.'

'OK, Khan, we'll do it your way,' Saleem sighed heavily, conceding defeat. His face brightened. 'What about roping them together?' Hurrying back to the tunnel, where they had left the saddlebags, he quickly reappeared, tying slipknots as he ran.

It was slow work. One by one Khan and Jack grabbed the children, keeping them still long enough for Saleem to slip the rope over their heads. Then pushing and pulling, they manhandled them out of the cage. Once out a few started to walk, the rest continued their ungainly hopping. They pulled against the rope, their heads twisting viciously from side to side, their mouths snapping like a bird's beak.

Footsteps echoed in the distance, breaking into a run. The boys froze, unable to move. In his mind's eye, Jack pictured guards crowding round the passage door; the lock – which Khan had opened through the magic of his fingers – turning silently, and the door opening. The footsteps sounded again, accompanied by loud shouts. The guards were running through the room of lights. Another door, then the words: *'They've gone! Inform the master.'*

More noise – more shouting – followed by a heavy thud and a high-pitched scream. Then silence.

'Saleem,' whispered Jack, 'down the tunnel – quick. We'll follow … *shush*, the door's opening.'

Jack and Khan flinched back into shadow, watching the door, between the room of birds and the lava bubble, swing open. It paused half-way, lingering silently for a moment or two as if to allow something to pass through, before slowly closing again. The hairs on Jack's neck stood up, his skin pricking painfully, as if a thousand needles were being jabbed into him. There was no sound. He poked his head a little further round the edge of the rock, but his view was impeded by the birds fluttering helplessly round the cage, seeking a space on the overcrowded perches. The faintest of sounds broke the suspense – a footfall. His heart stopped beating and he clutched at Khan's hand.

'*It's Sengila!* Oh, thank goodness.'

The huge beast came into sight. Gold-flecked eyes gazed into his and a voice broke into his thoughts. '*You must depart quickly, before the evil one comes.*'

'We're goin'' Khan replied, hearing the voice as clearly as Jack. 'Comin' Sengila?'

The deep voice came again. '*I go to wait for the master.*'

'Hang on a minute,' Jack ran after him. 'We need your help, first. Khan, hold that door open.' Heedless of the filth under his feet, Jack dived into the cage of birds followed by the lion. 'This lot's getting out too,' he yelled. 'Take cover, Khan, we're coming through.'

The birds rose up in panic as Sengila roared, loud echoes bouncing off the walls. As they came face to face with the lion they wheeled, flowing round and round the enclosed space until they discovered a change in the density of the air – no bars, simply a rectangle of space. Pushed by the birds behind, they flocked through the opening, stretching their wings as they flew, others herding after them. The air began to vibrate with the rush of wings. Scenting fresh air, they soared across the room in a thick black ribbon, sweeping a hair's-breadth from Khan standing in the open doorway. A black mass of bodies rose out of the lava cave into the dusky sky, like the black smoke of the Cardinals' conclave at the Vatican.

'And if Jacob's watching, he'll know we've been successful,' shouted Jack triumphantly. Sengila leapt up onto one of the cages and, springing over the edge of the lava bubble, disappeared after the birds. Hesitating only long enough to collect the saddlebags, the two boys headed into the safety of the darkened tunnel, turning for home.

Chapter Twenty-one

Mercedes the Warrior

Light-heartedly, the two boys jogged down the tunnel, quickly catching up with Mercedes and Saleem dragging the long line of bird-children behind them – Hamid and his friends urging them along like cattle.

'What was it, Jack?' called Mercedes.

'Sengila. He'll delay any pursuit as long as he can. But I wish Bud was here.'

'Well, he isn't. And if that madman does send someone, we're goin' to have to fight,' said Mercedes, a gleeful smile on her face.

'Not unless we're pushed into it,' growled Jack. 'You may like fighting, Mercedes, but I don't.'

Without warning, their ears were blasted by a shrill shrieking and, from the spot where the tunnel forked, a vast scaly head appeared spitting fire.

'*Blimey!*' shouted Khan. 'Why can't 'e just let us go 'ome!'

The animal surged forward, its clawed feet covered in chain mail, its sharp spines scraping against the tunnel roof, like chalk against a blackboard. Two eyes, wild and malevolent, squinted balefully at the little army of children.

They remained rooted to the spot, their hands covering their ears, their teeth grating as the unbearable noise continued.

'Anyone got a clue what this is?' Jack bellowed.

'I think 'e's out to scare us, Jack, an' stop us goin' on.'

'He's done that all right, Khan.'

'That's not what he means, moron,' yelled Mercedes. 'He means that weasel is tryin' to scare us with a mirage. He didn't have time to get anythin' real into the tunnel.'

'You mean we can just walk past it?' Saleem echoed, his voice quivering with fright.

'Anyone here stupid enough to have a go?'

'I will, if you like, Jack,' said Mercedes, not a bit put out by the roaring, spitting monster. 'Will you come with me, Khan?' She held out her stave. 'You can borrow this if you like.'

'Sounds like fun,' Khan grasped the heavy stick, testing its strength against the palm of his hand.

Hugging the wall, Khan and Mercedes edged cautiously towards the giant armadillo, their weapons at full stretch in front of them. Instantly, its beady eyes homed in on them and its jaw opened exposing a row of jagged teeth. It snapped viciously as if it were chasing flies. Belching loudly, a torrent of fire swooped down on them.

Khan flinched back as steaming air moved in front of his face, vivid memories of the wall of power overtaking him. Flames wrapped themselves round the two youngsters, the armadillo screeching so loudly it made their eardrums vibrate. Then they were through.

Khan laughed. 'I wish all Mendorun's villains were just 'ot air.'

'Wait here, I'll fetch the others,' said Mercedes, handing him her sword. She disappeared into the pall of smoke and flames. Khan waited, his eyes glued to the tunnel in front of him.

'You don't 'alf look funny with them kids,' he called, smiling his lop-sided smile, as Jack and Saleem appeared surrounded by a line of hopping and crawling children.

'He's not as good as Pops,' Mercedes retrieved her sword and sheathed it.

'No, but he won't stop there. We'd better get cracking, before he tries something really real,' said Jack.

They moved off again, the screeching of the dragon look-a-like abruptly switched off as the rock tunnel twisted like a corkscrew. Rounding a corner they found the bars of the portcullis looming through the darkness, the silhouette of the flatbed truck visible on the far side.

'Hurrah! We've made it.' Saleem dashed over to the gate climbing up on the bars; the little party of children clustering round him, as if they sensed they were at last free.

'*Shush!*' Jack waved his arms in the air. 'Khan, get that gate open fast. *Saleem, hang onto the kids.*'

Khan ran over to the huge wheel, studying it closely.

'What is it Jack?' Saleem jumped down from his vantage point, herding the line of children behind him.

'Can't you hear it? There's something tracking us.'

Mercedes calmly unsheathed her sword, handing Jack her stave.

'If it's what I think it is, we're going to need more than you and me.' Jack's voice faltered. His belly growled nervously, rumbling loudly.

'You worry too much,' she twirled her sword eagerly in a figure of eight.

Three figures brushed past them, darting haphazardly, as if searching for somewhere to hide.

'Hamid, come back?' Jack shouted after them. 'It's your only chance.'

'We're fighting with you, sir.'

The three children scurried back to the gate; Mina and Abdul clutching a length of heavy wood, Hamid a long metal bar.

'We ain't going to be captured again, sir,' he added defiantly.

'I told you, you worry too much,' Mercedes laughed gleefully.

The faint sounds from the tunnel turned into the panting and snarling of a pack of hyenas. They slunk into view – teeth bared.

'They real?' asked Jack his voice faltering. Trembling, he held the stave at arm's length, envying Mercedes her apparent unconcern.

'Yep,' replied Mercedes cheerfully. 'Pity Sengila isn't here, but isn't that always the way with Pops's beasts – like that poxy camel – never around when you need them. *Hi-yah*!'

Her sword flashed in time with Jack's stave blocking the headlong rush. A chorus of yelps filled the tunnel void as wood and steel landed on flesh and bone, the animals tossed back head over heels. Regaining their feet, they swung round heads low to the ground, their mouths and teeth dripping saliva. Their leader sprang towards Jack's throat, scenting he was the animal they had to cut out from the herd. Spinning on her heel, Mercedes ran it through, blood spurting from the gaping wound. She retrieved her sword, wiping the blood off on the animal's fur.

Jack felt rather than saw the next attack, almost touching the sweaty, drooling snout before his stave connected with its skull. It fell back whimpering, skulking into the tunnel behind. There came a screech of pain, a chorus of high-pitched yelps, and yet another dog fled; Khan and Saleem aiming stones with deadly accuracy. As light as a butterfly, Mercedes darted about sensing where she was needed most; her sword a blur of light. At Jack's side, the three youngsters worked together beating at any animal that came within range, until finally the last one fell bleeding and maimed on the ground.

'Thanks, Mercedes.' Jack stepped away from the heap of bodies. 'You're a great fighter.'

'I know.' Sheathing her sword, she gave him a friendly smile. 'That's why I get mad every time anyone tells me I can't do this or that 'cos I'm a girl.'

'I promise, you'll never hear that from me again; I'd be too scared.' He glanced down at his watch. 'It can't be! It's almost six. The sun will be setting.'

'Then we'd better get these kids back to Pops in a hurry.'

With a blinding flash of clarity, like the reflections of light from the sharp edges of Mercedes' sword, Jack understood what Jacob and Bud had tried to hide from him. 'He won't be there, Mercedes,' he said with absolute certainty.

'Of course he will, *won't he?*' she said, her eyes wide with alarm.

Jack buried his face in his hands and shut his eyes, willing his brain to work … to think. How could he have been so stupid … He should have guessed any plan Jacob made would include Bud.

Saleem ran up and pulled his arms down. 'Jack, Jack,' he hissed. 'What is it? You're scaring us. Are you hurt?'

'Bud knew,' Jack blurted out. 'Jeez! That's why he made such a fuss, he needed Bud with him.'

Without waiting to explain, he tore over to Khan already turning the handle to raise the portcullis, and leaned his weight on it.

'Quick, into the truck, there's no time to lose.'

The gate creaked to a standstill, Jack and Khan holding it steady. Abdul, Mina and Hamid quickly ducked through, taking some of the more able children with them, leaving Saleem and Mercedes to manhandle the tethered line onto the truck.

'You go first, Khan, I'll hold the gate.'

For a second it seemed as if Khan was about to argue. He shrugged and, dropping the handle, dived underneath the rigid squares of iron.

'Come on, Jack!' he shouted.

'*I'm not going!*'

'YOU'RE NOT WHAT!' yelled Saleem and Mercedes together. Leaving the children, they tore back to the gate.

'Jack, stop messin' about,' growled Khan.

'I'm going after Jacob,' Jack shouted and released the handle. For a moment the gate hung silently, its momentum suspended. Even now, Jack knew he had time to change his mind – and desperately, wanting to. Then, with a shudder, it hurtled downwards.

'Not wivout me ye're not.' Khan, as calm as ever, rolled under swiftly moving gate.

'KHAN!' screamed Mercedes, putting her hands over her eyes.

The wicked spikes of the portcullis crashed into place behind him.

'Jack! Khan! *This is madness*,' yelled Saleem angrily.

'Jack's mad. I'm only stoppin' to keep 'im out'a trouble.' Khan's face broke into a grin.

'You can't return to the fortress, Jack,' Mercedes stormed. 'That's just plain stupid. Get the gate open again and leave it to Pops.'

'*Pops* hasn't done a very good job so far, Mercedes,' Jack flashed back, aware his criticism of Jacob would start her steam rising. 'Mendorun continually out-guesses him. *And* he's all alone, he doesn't even have Bud. So I'm going.'

'He's got Sengila.'

'So what! Now, he's got me, too. And you're wasting time. I'm not changing my mind. So go.'

'Come on, Merk. You won't stop him. He's as obstinate as you when he wants to be, and that's saying something.' Leaping onto the flatbed, Saleem yanked the handle out of its socket shoving it into the slot on the far side. Slowly, the wheels began to move. 'See you back at the palace.'

Quickly gathering speed, the flatbed truck full of children disappeared round the bend and was lost to sight.

Slinging the saddlebags over his shoulder, Jack turned away from the gate. Then, skirting round the torn carcasses of their enemy, the two boys jogged slowly back towards the fortress.

Chapter Twenty-two

Sirius and Ghia

'*What is it wiv you, Jack,*' Khan grumbled. 'All ye do is spend yer time escapin' from the fortress, then gettin' back in again.'

'Said like that, Khan, I sound bonkers.'

'Well, I didn't say it, mate. You got a plan?'

'Not to get captured.' Jack slowed his pace to a walk, fearing another encounter with the screeching reptile. But the passage remained silent, the apparition vanished as swiftly as it had materialised.

Abruptly, they caught the sound of rocks being hurled through the air, as if a bomb had been detonated, followed by a series of explosions progressing up the tunnel towards them, like a giant in heavy boots.

'*Run, Khan!*'

The boys fled past the fork in the tunnel, the ominous sound increasing the speed of their flying feet. Khan, looking back, saw the tunnel disintegrate, dust and smoke billowing out over the running shapes.

'Great idea, Jack,' he gasped.

'Run – don't talk.' Grabbing Khan's arm, Jack forced him to keep pace with his own furious feet.

They burst out of the rock tunnel into the room of birds, silent and empty. The tunnel behind them collapsed like a house of cards, sealing off any escape through the mountain.

'What about Saleem and Mercedes?' Khan held his aching sides. 'Not used to runnin' like that,' he groaned.

'You'd better take up football then,' Jack said scornfully. He stared at the mountain of rock blocking the tunnel. 'Jacob or Mendorun?'

'Me monies on Jacob.'

'Mine too,' said Jack. 'So they're safe and heading for the palace. Jacob's just making sure Mendorun can't escape that way.'

'So now what? 'Ow do we get out'a this mess?'

Jack lifted the saddlebag from his shoulder. 'This is so weird. Jacob knew we would need them. But how?'

Carefully removing the wooden carvings, he opened the door to the lava bubble. The monster crows remained fast asleep under their gold light but the daylight had vanished; replaced by the warm darkness of early evening, a single star lighting the sky. Bending down, he placed the wooden statues under one of the oil lamps close to the door.

He waited, never tired of witnessing the magic that allowed the small shadows to grow and expand, becoming alive. This time, however, instead of the sneering features of the camel, there was a rustle of feathers and bright eyes – fiercely gazing over a curved beak – studied the two boys.

'What are you called?' Jack said boldly.

'Sirius. My name is Sirius, Earthling.' The eagle's voice was deep and clear, like the open sky. It rustled its feathers, a gleaming circlet of silver clasped round its neck.

'Sirius, I need your great wings to carry me to find Jacob, the master,' Jack said, politely. 'Will you do this?'

'I am to serve you, whatever your wishes, Earthling.' The majestic head bowed, its eyes proud and independent, as if it were guardian of all the secrets of nature.

'And your friend?'

The deeply resonant voice answered him. 'That is my mate, Ghia.'

Ghia gazed through Jack as if she was reading his thoughts. She freed her wings from the wall, yearning to stretch them and fly up into the clouds. There was a rasping of beaks. The two birds stepped clumsily from the shadow of the wall and began to groom their feathers. Fully formed, they were both taller and stronger than the two boys gazing up at them. Khan stared in disbelief at the claws stretched out on the floor, twice the size of his own feet.

They hopped away from the restraining wall, their gait ungainly and awkward, their eyes gleaming with lust as they felt the breeze on their feathers; the open air a tantalising prospect for such wild things, caged in wood for such a long time.

'Climb on our back, Earthling, for we must be free, we cannot wait.' The proud eyes flashed impatiently.

'They safe?' whispered Khan.

Jack nodded. 'Scary though, but they'll get us out of here.'

He stretched up to grasp the bird's neck, flinching as Sirius dragged the sharp edge of his beak across his shoulder.

'Will I hurt you, climbing on your back?' he said.

Sirius declined to reply, his gaze almost pitying. Grasping the silver collar, Jack pulled himself up onto the broad feathery back, sitting astride the shoulders.

There was a rush of air and then he was airborne, the massive wings beating strongly to gain height, decelerating to cruising speed as the mountain dropped away below them, a dense mass of shadow in the moonlit sky.

For a few moments Jack felt all his troubles vanish, the clean air blowing them away, content to enjoy the exhilarating sense of freedom. Strangely, he wasn't in the least bit scared; not even bothering to hold the silver collar, as layer after layer of feathers closed in around him, gripping him firmly. However terrifying Jacob's beasts appeared, he knew they would guard him with their lives.

'We give thanks to the Gods for our liberty, Earthling.' The deep voice of Sirius woke Jack from his trance. The pair of eagles soared high into the sky, as if they wanted to touch the heavens. 'Where do you wish us to take you?'

'Can you fly over the mountain?' Jack said. 'I want to discover what's happening.'

Sirius dipped his beak in acknowledgement, his wings outstretched and hardly moving, floating in the thermals. The pockets of warm air lifted them higher and higher into the night sky, grazing past the wakening stars.

Below them lay the earth, mapped out in a patchwork of paths, fields and mountains. In the distance, the doll-size silhouette of the palace of Prince Salah. From the sky the entire kingdom was visible; the valley oasis protected from the outside world by mountains, but not from the evil practised by Mendorun. Immediately below them lay the great mountain range, under which they had walked to rescue the bird-children. A natural barrier to all but the foolhardy, with its hilly slopes that quickly changed into precipitous cliffs, festooned with crags and escarpments like the serrated edge of a knife. Nestling into its south-eastern slopes was the small town of Tigrit, while to the north and west an occasional beam of light betrayed the position of Asfah, where Jack's adventure had begun. The massive walls of the fortress ranged into view, brooding and sulky under the night sky.

Ghia floated alongside, with Khan safely perched among her feathers. 'Jack,' he shouted, 'Is Jacob there?'

'No, not yet. Wait! What's that?'

Lights had sprung up all over the fortress, wiping away the darkness. It was extraordinary how easy it was to spot movement on the ground, even at such a height. Figures, foreshortened by the distance, hurried from the underground caves. Smoke billowed from the tunnel entrance as the face of the mountain slipped, nose-diving into the ground, spewing rocks into the air with the force of the blast.

'Jacob's destroyed the fortress,' Jack shouted joyfully.

Only Khan turned his head to show he'd heard, the majestic eagles ignoring the ramblings of the earthlings.

'That's the end of the birds and about time, too.'

The great gate, with its iron portcullis, opened and Mendorun's soldiers ran out. At cloud height there was no sound to accompany their panicky dashing across the courtyard. The eagles descended slightly. Jack heard a sharp click of metal on stone, and the sound of horses' hooves pawing the ground. Three animals waited impatiently in the courtyard, while a steady stream of men – laden with bundles and boxes – surged through the gate, heading for the desert track that led to Asfah.

A pall of smoke hung over the fortress, the gates wide open as if expecting visitors. For a moment or two nothing happened. Then, carried on the breeze, came the sound Jack had been dreading; the ringing noise of a camel's harness. Someone was approaching. The noise stopped and a lone figure appeared at the edge of the standing stones, where the valley road petered out. Jack's heart sped up, thumping noisily, as he recognised the tall, silent, bearded shape, his eyes kept hidden from the world to conceal their aura of power.

'It is the master. We must go to wait upon him.'

'No, Sirius,' Jack shouted. 'You may be needed to save his life.'

'Save his life, Earthling. He is in no danger.' The eagle swivelled his head eyeing the boy pityingly.

'Not yet, but there's danger looming close by. Can't you feel it, I can? It's been too easy. *Please,* Sirius,' he begged.

The eagle considered Jack's words, calling out to Ghia in their own language; a language of wild, empty sounds, reminding Jack of vast, echoing canyons through which rivers had run million of years before.

The proud head turned, its eyes gleaming with untamed ferocity.

'Ghia recalls what occurred long ago. She says it may well happen again and to watch closely. But be warned, Earthling, we can look into your heart and will follow only if you speak truth. If the master falls into danger, we wait for no earthling to speak.'

The ground in front of Jacob shifted, moving uncertainly like quick sand, and the firewall erupted, its flames creating an impenetrable barrier between him and the fortress walls. The great skeletal head of Sebola materialised, looming over the fierce reds of the inferno, a waterfall of flame gushing from its eye sockets.

At the same moment Mendorun appeared on the deserted ramparts. Great golden robes clothed the sorcerer from head to toe and, behind him, reared his shadow. Like the sand monster, it had grown into a towering figure of menace, the gold of its robes emitting a glow which enveloped even the living sorcerer.

'*Ah! It is the evil one,*' screeched Sirius, his wild cry echoing through the silent sky.

'You recognise him, Sirius?'

'Yes, Earthling. The marks scarred into his face. It was I that put them there.'

All of a sudden, Jack felt scared again, very scared, as if something unspeakable was about to happen and he was being warned.

He touched the bird's head. 'Sirius, with your eyes you can spot a mouse move, I am relying on you.'

'Yes, Earthling.'

'Tell me about Mendorun?'

'There was a great battle, one the master could not win for he had little power. All that was left to him had been bartered for the life of the child. The evil one had first destroyed my master's family and then his army. They were all dead, all but Ghia and I. The master lay on the ground at his feet, begging him to spare the child. But the evil one has no heart. He crowed his triumph, raising his arms to slay them both. "*I have rid the world of all but one,*" he gloated. "*Now it is your turn. Finally, the line will be extinct.*" As his arms reached into the sky I struck with all my might. The blow knocked him backwards and the lightning bolt, destined for my master and the child, spun harmlessly away. Ghia took the child and I the master, carrying them to our eerie on the mountain top where no earthling can reach us, and where we can watch the earth move through the heavens.'

'And the child?' Jack asked breathlessly.

'It was a girl child.'

Mercedes, thought Jack. *Sirius and Ghia saved Mercedes.*

'The master is moving,' Sirius called out. His great wings stirred lazily into motion, dropping even nearer the earth.

A great roar filled the night sky. It echoed against the circle of mountains, magnifying the sound until even the residents of Asfah could have heard it.

'*You!*' Louder than any human voice, like thunder rumbling, it flowed from the mouth of the sand monster making the very air shiver with fear.

Jacob seemed unperturbed. 'You are surprised?' he called, his voice crystal clear, as if he was calling upon the heavens to witness his words.

'Disappointed, perhaps, that you are still living.' Jack recognised the silent, menacing tones of Mendorun's voice.

'Do I call you Mendorun?'

'What you will, cousin.'

Cousin, exclaimed Jack silently.

'It matters not what you call me, since you will not live long enough to repeat it.'

'You mistake, Mendorun. Now, it is my turn.'

Jacob's hands opened. There came a flash of light from the small box which lay on his palm. The sky darkened. Storm clouds crashed together with a thunderous noise and bolts of lightning hurtled towards Sebola's head, and the fire raging beneath it. The firewall sizzled, blackening under the deluge. From every angle, spears of light struck the head of the sand monster.

Cracks appeared in the cone of sand, large pieces breaking off. Then, an avalanche of sand flooded downwards.

Jack stared at Mendorun. Unmoving, he seemed unconcerned by what was happening.

Why was Mendorun taking no notice? Why wasn't he using his power to prevent the destruction of the sand monster? Suddenly Jack knew.

'*It's a trick*,' he yelled at the top of his voice. '*It's a trick!*'

Chapter Twenty-three

The Fiery Furnace

The sound echoed round and round the mountain crags, unheard by the people below. There was nothing left of the wall, nor the monster, only scorched earth. Jacob took a step forward across the smouldering rocks.

'NOOOOooooooooooooo!'

Khan and Jack shouted at the same time, but the sound never reached, blown away by the lingering storm clouds.

Mendorun raised his hands so quickly that the movement was blurred. A web, which had lain unnoticed beneath the embers of the fire wall, sprang up. In a haze of speed, its threads spun round and round, obscuring Jacob's body – his arms pinned to his sides, immovable and powerless.

Jack wanted to reach down and tear the threads away but, like Jacob, he too was helpless. He closed his eyes unable to bear the sight.

'You have greater power than I anticipated, Mendorun.' Jacob's voice sounded quite calm.

Mendorun drew himself up, even the soft tones of his voice overwhelming the amphitheatre of rocks behind him.

'I have spent years learning how to create creatures to rival your familiar and you have destroyed them all. As you know to your cost, cousin, I will not be thwarted. *Failure only serves to make me more determined to succeed.* I decided to trap you.' He laughed. 'It was not easy creating such magic. Even I can tell from your aura that you have gained much knowledge. Enough, perhaps, to give me warning of your approach – but you still remain weak. This is good because the net has taken all my power. See, I am as helpless as a babe in arms.' Mendorun raised his arms to the sky laughing again, a silent mirthless laugh.

Despairing, Jack listened to the words. There had to be something he could do.

'But you are even more helpless,' Mendorun continued. 'You cannot move to break the threads, only I *Mendorun the invincible*. And once you are dead, my power will return – twofold. For is it not my right to garner the skills of the vanquished. And you, my pathetic cousin, will be the vanquished.'

The ground in front of Jacob, occupied by the standing stones, split open as if someone had used an axe to it. A wide chasm formed below the walls of the fortress and, from its depths, thick tendrils of steam arose.

'Sirius,' Jack wasn't sure why he whispered, no one on the ground could possibly have heard him. 'What is that?'

'It is the fire from the earth's centre, Earthling. We go now.'

'*Wait!*'

'*Earthling!*' The cry of the eagle echoed plaintively through the empty air. 'It will be too late to save him.'

Jack glanced at Khan, his expression pleading.

'Yeah I'll try, OK.' Khan answered Jack's unspoken question.

'Have you power enough left to cast me into the furnace?' the voice of Jacob called, from within the depths of his black shroud.

'Perhaps!'

Then the world exploded – everything happening at once.

The eagles dived before Jack's brain could even flash the instruction into words. The ground roared towards them, air screeching and hissing with the force of their dive. Jack gripped the silver collar as if his life depended on it. His cheeks were pulled tightly back with the speed; the skin on his face threatening to rip open and expose the muscle underneath, while the ground continued to hurtle towards them.

Mendorun laughed triumphantly. He raised his arms, solid air moving from his fingertips like a cannon ball. It hit Jacob squarely so that he overbalanced, toppling towards the furnace in the bowels of the earth. Abruptly Mendorun's laugh was choked off, as the tawny shape of the lion sprang on him from the cliff above.

Hardly conscious, Jack forced his head round to look at Khan; his hands creating a speeding pathway through the air. One of the standing stones fell across the chasm, Jacob falling heavily onto it. Next second, the eagles were tearing at the net, their beaks piercing the black webbing. Then, with their feathers singed from the heat, they were flapping away from the burning furnace.

They landed on the rocky slope of the mountain side. Jack rocked backwards as the ground tilted and swung around his shattered senses.

'Khan?'

'OK – I feel sort of …' Khan's body slipped down from the back of Ghia, tumbling into a motionless heap on the ground.

A gun shot rang out, following by yelping cries.

Leaving the eagles to release Jacob from his black shroud, Jack tore back towards the fortress and across the stone spanning the great crack in the earth. He was concentrating so hard that he failed to notice the fiery furnace beneath him, snapping at his heels, Mendorun's final piece of evil.

He burst through the gates and up the steps to the ramparts, where a moment ago Mendorun had been triumphant. The body of the lion was sprawled across the ground. Below him, stretched out on the courtyard floor, was the torn and bloody form of Mendorun, his gold robes in shreds where the teeth and claws of Sengila had savaged him.

Saladin appeared laden with bags and packages which he slung over one of the horses. He crossed to the battered body of the sorcerer and, hauling it upright, dragged it anyhow into the saddle like a bundle of rags. Jack gasped in disbelief as he saw the flicker of movement, the fingers bending as the corpse's hands clutched the reins. Saladin climbed ponderously into the saddle and, clicking his heels against the flanks of the horse, moved slowly away; the two animals with their burdens following.

Sengila was panting heavily, his eyes closed in pain. Crouching down, Jack searched his pockets for a hankie, attempting to staunch the blood oozing from the wound in his chest, where Saladin had shot him.

Then, furiously angry, angrier than he'd ever been in his life, he tore after the horses. He stumbled down the steps towards the fortress gates, shouting loudly.

'SALADIN, YOU MURDEROUS THUG. YOU'VE KILLED MY FRIEND.'

He had been heard. Saladin pulled his horse to a standstill. He sat back in his saddle, fixing his black, soulless eyes on the angry boy.

'Let me guess. It is once again the footballer, Jack Burnside. If I had been a gambling man, I would have won my bet that you were part of this little charade. Your impertinence never ceases to amaze me.'

He set his horse in motion again. Miserably, Jack followed in their wake, aware there was nothing he could do. They would escape – but it was all wrong, they shouldn't go free. As they approached the standing stone over the chasm, an escape route provided by Khan's hands, Saladin slowed allowing the other two horses to precede him. As if he had left something undone, he pulled his horse to a halt. He swung round to face the boy, standing ten metres behind him.

'This is how I deal with impertinence.'

He raised his pistol. Jack stared in amazement. He had never before seen a real gun and its black muzzle held him captive, his legs unable to move. He watched transfixed as Saladin pulled back the trigger.

Then a patch of innocent moonlight turned into a familiar shape, the sneering, bad tempered, moody figure of the camel – his best friend Bud.

'*May the Gods curse you for what you did to the children and Prince Salah*,' he spat.

With the most vicious kick Jack had ever witnessed, he connected with Saladin knocking him out of the saddle, the shot spinning harmlessly into space. For a second Saladin hung there, clawing at the edge of the standing stone. Mendorun never looked up. Instead his feet moved sluggishly in the stirrups, urging his horse forward. With a scream, Saladin disappeared.

Jack turned, walking slowly across the courtyard and up the steps to Sengila's side. His legs gave way and he collapsed onto the ground. He stayed there, his hand on the lion's mane – too exhausted even to stand up, even to realise they had triumphed. It was enough they were alive.

Chapter Twenty-four

Rabat

Rob, his voice shrill, sounded despairing. 'I tell you, he's down by the pool.'

'We've checked – twice.' The exasperated tones of the team coach could clearly be heard through the closed bedroom door.

Jack laughed gleefully. Grabbing a magazine from the bedside table, he ran out onto the balcony. Hurling himself into one of the long sun-loungers, he opened the magazine pretending to read. He felt filthy. Glancing down, he saw that he looked filthy. Bud had dashed through the night sky, holding time suspended, so Jack could get back before Barney called the police. And, by the sounds of it, he had arrived in the nick of time. Obviously, Rob and Andy had been fighting a rear-guard action for some hours – well, he'd owe them big time.

'In fact we've checked everywhere and no one appears to have seen Jack for two whole days.'

The doors opened and a delegation surged in. Fronting it were Peter Barnabus, Mr Woods, Rob and Andy, closely followed by the entire team led by Tim and Petey – his quiff now dyed black.

'Haven't seen who for two days?' called Jack from the balcony.

Behind the broad shoulders of Barney, the expression on Rob and Andy's face nearly sent Jack into fits of laughter. Their mouths gaped open, their eyes bulging out on stalks like some species of codfish.

'*Where've you come from?*' Barney demanded.

'Nowhere, why?'

'You weren't here when we checked half an hour ago,' Tiger's dad said.

'No, I popped down to buy some chocolate.' Jack flourished the bar he had snatched from his bedside cabinet. 'Why?'

'You've been missing for two days. No one's seen you anywhere.'

'*Missing!* How could I be missing? I had a bad foot remember.' Jack shrugged nonchalantly, his face a picture of innocence. 'It's a big hotel and you told me to have a holiday, so I kept out of the way.'

'And off your foot, I hope. How is it by the way?'

'Better – it's great – look!'

Jack leapt to his feet, running on the spot. *Crutches! Oh blast!* He carried on jogging, hoping Barney wouldn't ask for them back – *because they would stay missing.* If he remembered correctly, they were in pieces last time he saw them, smashed to smithereens by the soldiers who had invaded Jacob's tent.

'OK! OK! That's enough. Report for training in the morning and I'll get the doctor to check you out. I don't know what you've been up to but have a shower, for pity's sake, you smell.'

Barney pivoted on his heel and marched out, followed by Mr Woods, still glancing suspiciously round the room, his parental-antennae alerting him that something was wrong but unable to spot what it was.

'Where …' began Tim eagerly.

'Later,' growled Rob and slammed the door in his face. He leaned back against it to stop anyone getting in. '*Where have you been?*' he hissed.

'You promised to be back hours ago,' said Andy, looking furious. 'We were nearly on a plane out'a here 'cos'a you.'

'I'm ever so sorry. But it couldn't be helped. I'm here now and I'm famished. I don't think I've eaten anything for days.'

'OK, we'll talk over dinner but shower – Barney's right – you stink. You smell like you've bin buried alive,' said Andy cooling down, now he knew he wasn't going to be punished for Jack's sins.

Jack laughed and headed for the shower. 'Rob – I've got some bad news.'

'What?'

'My foot's fit for the match tomorrow,' he called from the bathroom, busily soaping himself all over. 'I'm sorry but you won't get a game.'

'*Oh yes, I will,*' his friend yelled back. 'Gary's broken his collarbone falling off a camel.'

'Falling off a camel! How did he do that?'

'Dunno. Showing off, I guess – you know Gary.'

'It was great.' Andy laughed. 'Wish you'd bin there to have a go. They're real cool animals.'

'I guess.' Jack hastily dried himself, grinning at his reflection in the mirror as he combed his wet hair. 'Come on, let's go to dinner and you can fill me in on everything that's happened while I've been away.'

***

Jack pulled out his clean shirt and shorts, laundered by the hotel since their last match, and changed ready for the game. It was as if a huge weight had been lifted off his back. He'd had two great sleeps – going to bed early on Sunday night and having a siesta Monday straight after lunch. He'd eaten huge quantities of food, taken several showers, and had played a practise session, which had finally removed any lingering effects from his exertions of the past three days.

Once again there had been little time for talking, or celebrating, before Bud had whisked him back to the hotel in Rabat; time spinning backwards to allow them arrive immediately after sunset, when the camel was again free to roam the skies. Unfortunately, despite Bud's manoeuvring, it had been almost too late; a second or two more and Barney would have raised the alarm.

And that was almost the only thing he had managed to ask Jacob, before leaving. They had finally found themselves alone after the jubilation of the previous few hours, with the realisation that Mendorun's power had been destroyed – and with it all danger to the kingdom.

By the time the weary and injured combatants reached the palace, where Saleem and Mercedes were anxiously waiting, it was late. Overhead the eagles, able to soar to the stars while the moon was in the sky, accompanied the small party. Bud, aware that his power would shortly be called upon to transport Jack back to his world, insisted on carrying the street-boy whose magic had saved his master. While Khan, his face exhausted-looking with pits of blue shadow ringing his eyes, continued to protest to anyone who would listen, that he was fine really.

'The children?' Jack asked.

Saleem smiled. 'The palace has never been so full.' He gazed anxiously at Khan.

'I'm all right,' protested Khan.

'My Lord Saleem, I must attend to Sengila. Make sure that the young Khan goes straight to bed.'

'Don't worry, Jacob, I'll sit on him if I have to. Jack, will you be back to say goodbye?'

'After I've checked on Sengila.'

He and Jacob, riding the camel that had carried Jacob into Mendorun's lair, made their lumbering way back to the cave, where Jacob had left the injured lion, the camel's splay feet making little sound on the sandy track.

'Why couldn't we have used magic, Jacob?' said Jack. 'It would have been quicker.'

'Alas, there is no power left in my hands,' Jacob admitted, bringing the camel to a halt outside the invisible cave. 'Aren't you also sickened by the harm sorcery has caused us all this day?' he added sadly.

'But Khan will be all right?'

'Of course, he is well enough even now, but weak. The effort of making the stone fall was very great. I will confine him to bed for a day or two, to be certain there are no ill-effects. Have you said your goodbyes to him?'

Jack grinned. 'He was all set to return with me to England. I told him to stay. Do you think he will?'

'At least until we have restored the children to their right minds.' Jacob crossed the floor, staring down at the injured animal. 'After that who knows?'

'But you can cure them?'

'With great care, they will all be returned safely to their homes before many moons have passed. And there will be such rejoicing.'

Sengila lay quietly, his great eyes closed in pain. Jack crouched down stroking the lion's head. 'He won't die will he, Jacob? He's lost a lot of blood. I couldn't bear it if he died.'

'No, the bullet is deep and may lame him slightly,' Jacob delicately prodded the shoulder muscle searching for the bullet. 'It would have killed an ordinary beast, but Sengila is not ordinary. And had it not been a weapon created by sorcery, it would not have been such a grievous wound. Fortunately, it will take much evil to kill our friend here. Indeed, like you, I could not bear to lose him.'

As if he had heard, the gold-flecked eyes opened gazing up at his master for a moment before closing again.

There was silence as Jacob probed deeper and deeper into the wound, Jack fascinated by his skill.

'There,' Jacob sat back, his hands covered in blood. 'At last, I have the bullet.' He held up the dark casing between the ends of a pair of forceps. 'We will leave him to heal. But first, a few stitches.' Using a type of large darning needle, he quickly sewed the lion's mangled fur back together. 'Help me put on a bandage to stop the bleeding.'

Jack held the cloth in place with one hand, lifting the heavy front paw with his other. The lion's claws were sheathed harmlessly within their rough pads, the same claws that had so mercilessly torn Mendorun apart. Jacob skilfully wound the bandage across the lion's chest and round his shoulder, to hold the pad in place.

'Jacob? How did Bud arrive in time to stop Saladin shooting me?' Jack asked as Jacob stood up, clearing away the blood-soaked rags. 'I left him in the tunnel.'

'A precise manipulation of time …' Jacob replied calmly, pouring water in a bowl for the lion to drink. 'Which, thanks to the Gods, worked. The animal must be improving at long last,' he added, his tone of voice once again sounding gloomy.

'Jacob?' Jack swallowed loudly, the words stuck in his throat.

'Yes, my Lord Burnside?'

'I'm sorry.'

'Sorry!' exclaimed the sorcerer. 'You are sorry – for what? I do not understand – you and Khan *saved my life*. It is I who should apologise, for I doubted that the children could be rescued. Once again, you have proved me wrong.'

'But I took Bud when you needed him.'

'Ah!' Jacob sat down opposite the boy, his hand on Sengila's head. 'That too was my fault or so that curs-ed beast tells me. He said I should have trusted you.'

'Yeah – you should,' Jack said, feeling better about things already. 'But that won't happen unless I use a knife to dig the secrets out of you, like that bullet.'

Jacob gave a brief smile.

'But I don't understand why you put *your* life on the line, like that.'

'To strip Mendorun of all his power. To beat me to the ground every last vestige of his power was bartered. At that moment Sengila could have destroyed him, while I used the box to extricate myself. Sadly, I under-estimated Mendorun's cunning and my hands were bound.'

'You nearly died.'

'But as you see – I did not.'

'He called you cousin?'

'Indeed, he was my cousin. We spent our childhood together, growing up in the same village. Sadly, he took to the dark side and destroyed the family in order to acquire their power. I tried to stop him and failed.'

'Sirius told me.'

'Ah, yes, my loyal friends Sirius and Ghia. But all that is in the past and Mercedes and I survived. Come, my Lord Burnside, it is gone time for you to leave.'

Jack ignored him, determined to achieve at least a few answers; the mysteries stacking up like a pile of CD's gathering dust.

'Does Mendorun's power go to you?'

'Will he live? You said he was scarcely alive when Saladin put him on the horse.'

'Well, if he dies will it come to you?'

Jacob nodded and, rising to his feet, ushered the boy from the cave.

'We have to go, time is passing so quickly – it is late into the night and that curs-ed animal can only help you while it is dark.'

'But you haven't answered all my questions.'

Jacob glared. 'If I answer all your questions, you will have none to ask next time we meet.'

'Some chance of that,' replied Jack gloomily. 'There's at least a million, and you only answer one at a time. But please answer me this before I explode.'

Jacob dragged the reluctant camel down the slope, forcing it to kneel. 'About my metamorphosis into a different person, my Lord Burnside?'

'How did you ...' began Jack. He laughed. Jacob was like Mendorun. He could also read minds but in a good way. He climbed up onto the back of the camel, settling himself against its hump, Jacob in his usual place on the shoulders. The bells on the camel's harness broke into their melodious ringing sound as the camel began to move, heading for the palace.

'But you already have the answer.'

'Well, I guessed that Jacob the merchant was a disguise, to hide you from Mendorun. But the other person appeared even before Mendorun was destroyed. That's the bit I don't understand.'

'Indeed, it was more than a new identity. I had so little power left it was useless. To protect Mercedes, I had to become someone without power, even my aura was removed so no trace of it was left. Anyone interested in pursuing me would believe I had died – as indeed did Mendorun. And so I became a simple merchant. Over the years the power began to re-assert itself, forced to do so by the danger to my good friend, Prince Salah. Recently, it has become impossible to maintain my new identity when called upon to use my powers.'

The lights of the palace came into sight, the gates opening as the guards spotted the lone camel with its riders.

'I wish I didn't have to go,' Jack sighed. 'Will I see you again?'

'Of course, and sooner than you think.'

Chapter Twenty-five

The Final Game

The little line of boys clattered down the steps and out onto the pitch, their opponents alongside them. A team from Marrakech, they were reported to be considerably superior to the Rabat footballers they had beaten the previous week.

The game started tentatively, both sides unsure of their opponents and feeling their way, with shocks a plenty happening in the first ten minutes; players kicking out wildly, desperate to gain the upper hand.

Tim called his team to heel, calming them down, getting nervous defenders into place, as attacks from all sides were thrown at them from the more experienced Marrakech side. They held on minute by minute, struggling to keep the ball in play. The home crowd's partisanship made their task even more difficult, vociferously cheering every attack so loudly that the defenders began to lose heart, overwhelmed by the noise.

A miskick finally brought Jack into the game. He grabbed at the chance wheeling the ball out to Tim, already sprinting down the pitch towards the Marrakech goalkeeper. He passed back to Jack, as one of the defenders caught up with him. Jack collected the ball cleanly against his right shin, letting it drop down onto his instep. Left back closed in on him, a purposeful look on his face.

Now or never, Jack took the kick, the ball thundering towards the goal. It clipped the right post, ricocheting harmlessly over the top and out of play. The linesman waved his flag and the goalkeeper sprinted across to collect it.

A long kick returned the ball back up the pitch; the Marrakech strikers immediately besieging Andy in goal, his plump face wearing an expression of extreme indignation at their cheek. Launching himself on the ground, he grabbed the ball from under the heels of the attack, sending it high in the air to safety.

'OK. Not bad but not good either,' Barney greeted his team as they flocked into the locker room at half-time, the score a tantalising nil-nil.

'Tim, you did some good work holding the team together. They're tough, better than the Rabat lot. Their strikers are good – fast – which makes for a lot of pressure on you, Rob, and you too, Petey. You did especially well, Andy. Well done for keeping your cool.'

Barney glared round at his team. 'But he's your last resort, remember? There's four defenders in front of him and, if necessary, four more in front of that. Half of you are standing around as if you've got glue on your boots. How can you protect your goal unless you move. Remember, *float like a butterfly sting like a bee*. Who said that?'

'Muhammed Ali,' came a chorus of groans, since Barney repeated the phrase at least once a week.

'And who was he?'

'Heavyweight Champion of the World,' groaned the chorus obediently.

'You bet your life he was, and the finest fighter on two feet we'll ever see. You've watched the video, so you've no excuse for gluey feet. Jack?'

'Yes, Barney,' said Jack, aware of what was coming.

'Your kicking's spot on – except you've chosen the wrong sport. You should be playing rugby – never seen better, if you're wanting to fly one into the air.'

Jack grinned at Barney's sarcasm, saying nothing.

'Right lads, you've held them so far. Second half, I want to see you lot defending as if your life depended on it. *You,*' he glared belligerently at his midfield section, '*are going to play out of your socks for me, OK*! I expect your shadowing to be so good you won't need the forwards, and they can take that ball up the pitch and score me a goal. That's all I want – one goal. And *keep those feet moving.* Off you go – good luck.'

The team trundled back out, listening to their captain's last minute instructions.

It was hard, the opposing team pressing and pressing, the ball mostly in their half, forcing the four defenders to jump through hoops to keep it out of the net. Andy, red-faced and never stationary for a second, bellowed furious instructions to anyone slow to pick up an incoming kick.

Jack and Marco dropped back, in the hope that a loose ball would come their way so they could send it down the pitch into their half.

'Eh you, slow coach,' yelled a voice from the crowd.

Jack, out near the boundary on the right wing, glanced over his shoulder wondering where the sound was coming from.

'Thought ye said ye could run!' the voice called again.

Momentarily taking his attention off the game, Jack peered into the crowd. Pressed up against the low barrier, a boy in jeans and T-shirt grinned at him – a lop-sided grin!

'*Khan!*' Jack spotted two other jeans-clad teenagers shouting and waving at him – Saleem and Mercedes. And *Jacob*! He gasped as he saw the rich cream silk of the burnoose, covering the tall, silent figure – still Jacob, only a bit different.

'I SAY, JACK, YER COACH SAYS YOU CAN 'AVE DINNER WIV US,' Khan bellowed, 'IF YE CAN SCORE A GOAL, SO YE'D BETTA START RUNNIN'.'

A delighted smile broke out over Jack's face, just as the ball met

Andy's boot for the long pass, the ball dancing its way towards Jack on the wing.

'Can I run?' he laughed happily. He picked up the ball with his left toe. 'You betcha!'